If the sun doesn't kill you, the washing machine will

or My Real Life in the Middle East . . .

Peter Wood

KYLE CATHIE LIMITED

Peter Wood was born in London. This is his first book.

First published 1993 by
Kyle Cathie Limited
7/8 Hatherley Street, London SW1P 2QT

ISBN 1 85626 111 5 paperback

A Cataloguing in Publication record for this title
is available from the British Library.

Typeset by DP Photosetting, Aylesbury, Bucks
Printed and bound in Great Britain by
Cambridge University Press

Part lyrics of *My Way* reproduced on pages 184–5 by permission of
International Music Publications Ltd. © 1967 Barclay Morris Stc/Jeune
Musiques, France Intersong Music Ltd, London W1Y 3FA

This book is dedicated to the people of Qatar. To every last one of them. Apart, that is, from the officious medical officer at the eye test centre, and the two policemen who dumped me God knows where during the driving test, and the twerp of a manager of the electrical shop who sold me the non-existent cassette player, and the assistant at the doughnut shop which doesn't sell doughnuts, and the lunatic in a van who clobbered me from behind on the Doha ring road, and the manager of the local theatre where the only decent performance is given by the curtain, and the two nitwits at the Road Works Department who should retire down their own holes, and the idiot at the garage who . . . oh, forget the whole thing. It's dedicated to my mum.

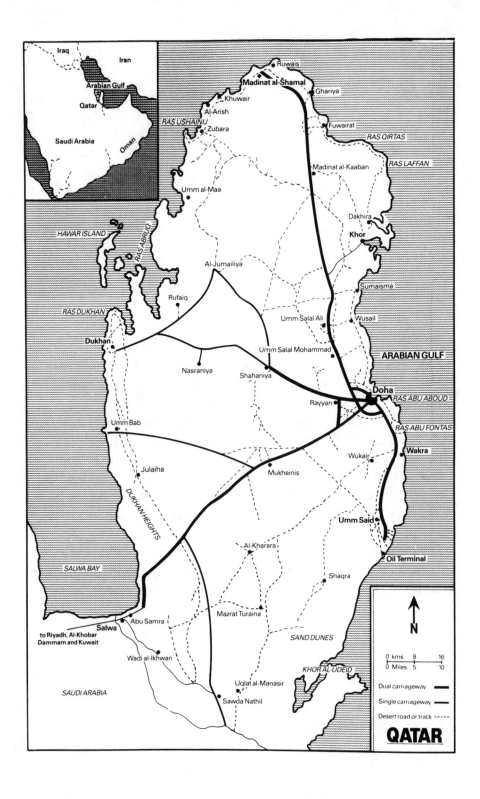

Iraq
Iran
Arabian Gulf
Qatar
Saudi Arabia
Oman

Ruwais
Madinat al-Shamal
Khuwair
Ghariya
Al-Arish
RAS USHAINIJ
Zubara
Fuwairat
RAS QIRTAS
Madinat al-Kaaban
RAS LAFFAN
Umm al-Maa
Dakhira
HAWAR ISLAND
Khor
RAS ABRUQ
Al-Jumailiya
Sumaisma
Rufaiq
RAS DUKHAN
Umm Salal Ali
Wusail
Dukhan
Umm Salal Mohammad
ARABIAN GULF
Nasraniya
Shahaniya
Doha
RAS ABU ABOUD
Rayyan
Umm Bab
RAS ABU FONTAS
Julaiha
Wukair
Wakra
Mukheinis
DUKHAN HEIGHTS
Umm Said
SALWA BAY
Al-Kharara
Oil Terminal
Shaqra
N
Mazrat Turaina
Abu Samra
Salwa
to Riyadh, Al-Khobar
Dammam and Kuwait
SAND DUNES
0 kms   8   16
0 Miles 5   10
Wadi al-Ikhwan
KHOR AL-UDEID
SAUDI ARABIA
Uqlat al-Manasir
Dual carriageway
Single carriageway
Sawda Nathil
Desert road or track

QATAR

Contents

1

Is this the end of civilisation as we know it?

I'd like, if I may, to change the subject.

It was last Tuesday I arrived in Qatar. The temperature was 127° Fahrenheit and it was National Pray For Rain Day. Looking around I could understand why. No fewer than five times that day, all Muslims would visit their mosques to pray for rain. Coincidentally, this was five times more often than it was likely to fall. A shame really. Such effusion of concentrated endeavour and not so much as a glimpse of an umbrella or a pair of galoshes to show for it.

I recalled that morning's conversation with the taxi driver on the way to London Airport.

'Qatar? That's one of them Gulf States innit? Where it's 'ot like Benidorm. And Sunday's on a Friday. And every-fings bleeding banned. First time is it?'

I nodded. 'I'll be working there three years.'

'Well, lucky you, mate. There's no booze y'know. And adultery's banned for women. And they 'ave to pray every morning facing America. Speaking for meself, I can't even face breakfast in the morning let alone America. Big place is it?'

'Qatar's about half the size of Wales. The capital, where most people live, is Doha. That's similar to Bradford.'

'Bradford? You'll find it a bit different from Bradford, mate. And I bet most of 'em can't even speak English proper.' Pausing a moment he then added, 'Well, I s'pose it's a bit like Bradford then. 'Ere, wanna 'ear a joke about Saddam Hussein and a camel?'

Wiping my brow, I wondered how long it would take to acclimatise to the heat. And my thoughts again returned to London.

'Two different worlds, mate. They'd chop yer whatsits off as soon as look at yer. Two different bleedin' worlds.'

And in a way he was right. Just eight short hours had transported me from the twentieth century back to an ancient desert land, where people still remember slaves, goats still roam the crowded streets, and Betamax is in.

If Qatar had a middle name, a prospect hampered by a self-evident numerical flaw, it would doubtless be forms. Not to suggest there's anything improper about forms, of course – in their right place. And that certainly appears to be Qatar. I'd been warned I was travelling to one of the world's foremost advocates of paperwork and early indications confirm this as not only correct, but probably a significant understatement. As I discovered last Tuesday.

Immigration control at Doha Airport confronted me with a line of ten channels, each of which led to a glass cubicle. Above five of the channels were signs instructing, 'For Arab Nationals Only'. The remainder specified, 'For Non-Arab Nationals'. Just one of the cubicles was manned, prompting a touch of homesickness as my local post-office came to mind.

To no one's surprise, the occupied cubicle was for Arab nationals and whilst they whizzed through at an average rate of twenty seconds per national, the rest of us, about 120 nons, milled around in general disarray. But not for long.

THE WASHING MACHINE WILL

Being the only European on the flight, I decided to serve Queen and country by taking the initiative and approaching a soldier who surveyed us with idle interest from outside a nearby office. Wearing an elegant uniform, he was armed with a machine-gun and moustache. But it was an ill-advised move. Some might say brainless.

Before completing three steps in his direction, the soldier's eyes locked firmly on to my tentative approach. Giving me a look like February he marched purposefully towards me, his gun and moustache poised ready for action. Failing miserably to melt back into the throng before being collared, I was presented with a mountain of landing cards half of which would have served the demands of well-nigh the entire population of China. Just great!

'All fill in please and form queue,' the soldier instructed, presumably placing me in charge. Casually he then indicated in the general direction of the cubicle and the lone imprisoned official.

In Qatar it's best to do what authority says. Even eating an After Eight mint can be risky without first checking your watch. I dispensed two dozen of the cards before dumping the remainder on the floor to stimulate self-service. It worked and we fashioned an erratic line of heterogeneous bodies, suitcases and passports. An Indian jammed next to me confided this would be the last time I saw anything resembling a queue in Qatar. I can believe it.

It took forty-five minutes to reach the cubicle as the twenty-seconds whizz-through factor for Arab nationals had increased to ten minutes for us. Frankly, the time was needed to complete the landing card which demanded enough information to write a biography. What is your name? What is your sex? What is your chosen religion? Are you married or happy? Has your budgerigar had any serious illnesses recently? Which eight records would you take on a desert island? If a train takes an hour to travel thirty miles between two stations and another takes forty minutes to travel the same distance in the opposite direction, when would the collision occur? The questions seemed endless.

Pushing the documents through to the entombed official, my initial impression was of a man who appeared to be interested in his work. Appearances, of course, are often deceptive and he stared immutably ahead. It seemed to be at a point just above my right shoulder and his glazed expression was of someone who'd spent the past six hours watching *Blind Date*. He was armed as well as bored.

My passport was punched with a startling array of stamps, one seemingly required for practically every week of my three years' stay. It was then pushed back through the partition and the landing card tossed casually into a cardboard box on the cubicle floor together with thousands of others. Who the hell's going to read all this junk? Maybe there's a department which analyses these things to produce the appropriate statistics. Whatever happens, I bet the information ends up at *Reader's Digest*.

Accepting my passport from the official, for the first time during our brief but purposeful acquaintanceship he looked directly at me, no doubt arranging the words 'off' and 'bugger' into a well-known phrase or saying.

'Good luck,' said the Indian I'd spoken to earlier. He was next in line. As I swung round to thank him, a soldier pushed me firmly the final few steps from Immigration into the Arrivals area. I entered Qatar backwards.

The day following my arrival, I began looking for accommodation. In a country where the relatively low value of land results in the range of available property being of a more spacious nature than could be contemplated in Britain, I began my task with enthusiasm.

I viewed various properties of varying standards and having disregarded the advice of those more experienced than myself, opted for an old stone villa with fourteen rooms. Fifteen if you count the dungeon at the back. Con-

structed on the edge of the desert just a few miles from
Doha, I found its location compelling. And with good reason.

Surrounded by a wall of fortress-like proportions,
entrance is gained through a pair of vast, fortified iron gates
which lead to an expansive courtyard that encircles the
building. The villa itself has a flat roof which accommodates
not only an observation lodge with viewing slats facing all
four directions, but also a flagpole and sundial. There is no
cannon. Otherwise its only external deficiency seems to be
turrets for tipping down boiling oil. So a dream home? Not
quite. The property also includes a selection of mainly
deranged livestock.

The pick of an unconvincing bunch are two sad-looking
cats with just three eyes, two ears and a tail between them.
They spend most of their day sitting motionless on the water
tank like a pair of Victorian gargoyles, watching five clack-
ing things on two legs which were probably once chickens,
and an unhinged duck which seems to think itself a chicken.

Which brings me to the goats. Their main daily pre-
occupation is devouring waste bins and parked cars in such
prodigious quantities the police have become involved.
Whenever they bound into sight, their guilty demeanour
suggests they've just undertaken something utterly reprehensible, which they usually have. Although only three of
them, it smells like many more.

The commotion emanating most hours of the day and
night from this tatty collection of cats, chickens and goats is
totally disproportionate to their size and station in life. I'd
been installed at the villa precisely two days when the first
complaint turned up. It was from next door. Judging by the
unseemly row they were creating at five o'clock this morning, God knows from where the next one's coming. Probably Bahrain.

Inside the villa, the fittings are of quite eccentric proportions, with the bed eight feet in all directions, the cooker big

enough to smelt lead, and the television about the size of Birmingham – although more pleasing to the eye. With its tiny screen and monumental old-fashioned cabinet, it wouldn't surprise me one scrap if there's a Chinese take-away inside.

And then there's the vacuum cleaner. In Britain a monstrosity of this size would require a heavy goods vehicle licence to operate and its awesome power has already proved an embarrassment when the six-piece suite in the lounge was abruptly reduced to five.

However, during my first few days of residence, a number of defects became apparent. These involved the majority of the fixtures and fittings on the premises. Of particular annoyance was the wardrobe door in the bedroom which continually opened itself – disconcerting at three o'clock in the morning. Then there was a mystery involving the cold-water tap in the bathroom. Whenever it was turned on, the hosepipe out in the courtyard immediately began spraying water in all directions causing deep emotional distress to the cats whose soporific existence was abruptly terminated. This was both perplexing and irritating as there was no apparent correlation between the tap and the hosepipe, and the need to trudge outside whenever I wanted to clean my teeth proved distinctly inconvenient. Not that the hot-water tap was any more effective, being astutely installed to deliver either a raging torrent or a dismal trickle, the choice being made by the tap. But all these complications became insignificant when compared to the dilemma I experienced with regard to the washing machine.

During my third day at the villa, I decided to test this machine which would inevitably be exposed to frequent use and even in 1965 would have been considered something of a relic. Make that 1865. Only marginally smaller than the Royal Albert Hall, it needs a stepladder to reach the controls at the top. It has eight washing programmes but lacks operating instructions, so setting it on programme one, I placed some old socks inside and put the machine into action to test it and establish the length of the programme. And aside from a noise level equivalent to Concorde flying over a Status Quo concert, it appeared to function correctly.

Examining its progress after what I considered a perfectly reasonable period of an hour, I found my socks still rotating happily together. Leaving them to it, I checked again some thirty minutes later but the machine was still not satisfied. By this time I was late for an appointment so I left it grafting away and decided to establish the programme length on another occasion.

Returning six hours later, I was astonished to find it still thundering remorselessly on. Clambering nimbly up the ladder, I checked the dial, and Christ! For motives which doubtless will never be adequately clarified, this gigantic contraption was systematically working through all eight programmes and displayed no imminent prospect of relenting. Whilst the obvious move at this stage would have been to disconnect the machine from the electricity supply, there was a large handwritten notice glued to the wall which warned, 'Under no circumstances switch off this equipment until washing programme completed'. So, as I saw the situation, it was going to take me between eight and nine hours every time I wanted to do any washing. But I must admit my socks were clean.

In an attempt to resolve these complications, last Saturday I visited the office of my landlord Mr Al-Khalifi – a sheik who's worth a camel or two. Having arranged for repair men to call the following day, I headed home, together with Vincent my intrepid local driver. Easier said than done.

It's relatively simple to lose yourself in Qatar with one heap of sand looking much like another. Consequently, it proved impossible to track down the villa. I knew it was somewhere around the southern outskirts of Doha and it hadn't appeared too demanding to locate four days previously when accompanied by Mr Al-Khalifi.

After almost an hour we admitted defeat and returned to the office of my landlord who agreed to despatch his maintenance supervisor with me for a familiarisation re-run. Within ten minutes we were hopelessly lost and had no alternative but to return in shame to the office. Having endured our embarrassed explanations, Mr Al-Khalifi sent his site foreman in a Range Rover to lead me home. But the vehicle promptly blew a head-gasket, compelling our immediate and inglorious return to base. Terrific! This was worse than opening the front door to a pair of Jehovah's Witnesses.

Remaining impassive as I appeared in his office for the third time in thirty minutes, my landlord listened as I recounted this latest misfortune. Giving a resigned sigh, he walked to the window and with a serene wave of the arm hailed two passing taxis, just like the Queen Mother would have done it. To the driver of the first he gave animated directions to my villa. The second was instructed to wait before taking him to a nearby mosque.

As the drivers lingered outside, Mr Al-Khalifi summoned the maintenance supervisor to his office and told us both to follow the taxi to my villa. Then in a swirl of sand he vanished inside the other waiting vehicle en route to calming prayers.

To our immense surprise, the supervisor, Vincent and I turned up at the local mosque. In his hurried exasperation, Mr Al-Khalifi must have dived into the wrong taxi. I didn't encounter him again that day, but suspect he may have been involved in the second blown gasket of the morning.

The following day, my landlord's maintenance operation swung into action. I assumed that over a period of days, maybe three or four men would visit, an electrician, a plumber and a carpenter – perhaps supplemented by an assistant. But no. They all arrived together in an old bus, just like a works outing. Seventeen of them in all – one to do the work and the other sixteen to watch. None of them spoke a word of English, and apart from blowing up the cooker it all went very smoothly.

The replacement cooker arrived this morning although the remains of the original one can still be seen on the kitchen ceiling. The workman left hospital today.

During my first night at the villa, I dreamt I'd been nominated as the number one contender to fight Mike Tyson. Strange.

2
Would David Attenborough please phone me immediately?

Qatar and I have now been together for two weeks and I can't help thinking the impact of our unholy alliance is somewhat greater on me than it is on Qatar. The relative opulence and discipline of the life to which I'd become accustomed in London has not proved ideal preparation for this. The deprivation here is greater than I'd anticipated. They don't even have New Improved Daz. My washing machine gets visibly perturbed when faced with wads of ordinary Daz being shoved down its throat. Little wonder it's neurotic. And the general tempo of life is perceptively more measured than in Britain. It takes a week in Qatar just to find someone to tell you it takes a month.

And I've swiftly identified the source of what's likely to become my paramount concern during the coming months. The weather? No. The lack of alcohol? No. The authoritarian way of life? No again. And it's not even the fact the hired car I've been given is beige. There are numerous things it's best not to do in Qatar and driving a beige car is one of them. With all this sand about it takes half the day to find it.

No, it's the livestock. On the day I arrived, Mr Al-Khalifi

gave smiling assurance this disparate collection would con-
certedly, and at all times, conduct themselves in a suitably
decorous manner. But events have proved otherwise and
complaints are pouring in. When we spoke this morning for
the fourth time on the subject, he continued to maintain the
innocence of his duplicitous treasures. Really? Without
wishing to appear in any way sceptical, such assurance is
like a Michael Fish weather forecast. You know you'd like to
believe it but you've heard it all before.

Where I've gone wrong I'm not sure. I treat them as
equals and gave each one its individual name to assist in
promoting self-confidence and esteem. But an ungrateful
element amongst them is abusing my altruistic intentions.

I gave copious thought to choosing the names, appreciating how crucial the choice could be, influencing their
whole approach to life. A wrong decision could provoke
consequences beyond description. Imagine calling a goat
Hilda, or a chicken Hot Pants. But my resolute endeavours
appear to have been misplaced and the equanimity for
which I'm justly known is being severely tested by several of
the blighters.

But not the duck. It's as good as gold. After deep thought
and analysis of its schizophrenic personality, I decided to
name it Duck, to give the poor thing a clear indication of its
true identity. It obviously hasn't a clue what it's doing in
Qatar most of the time but then, from my initial observations, neither do most of the people here. Quite how it came
to be in such a confused state and obvious need of psy-
chiatric treatment, I can't imagine. Maybe it had a disturbed
family background. Parents separated, duckling abuse. That
sort of thing.

The chickens I find a little irritating. For a start they're so
breathtakingly tatty I'd be surprised if they don't breach
international guidelines. They eat from dawn to dusk and
most likely all night as well. But they don't produce anything. Not a single egg between them in fourteen days.

Maybe it's too hot. Being city born and bred, I'm dismally inexperienced concerning matters of this complex and candidly rather delicate nature. I must remember to make enquiries at the British Embassy.

I've named each of them after a different member of Status Quo. Not only because I've a sneaking regard for the group, but because my managing director in London considers both Status Quo and any random selection of chickens to be of comparable musical ability. Mind you, he is French.

The cats are proving something of a dilemma. One of them I've called Scarface – which seemed a good idea at the time. In fact I've named them both Scarface. It saves arguments. Whilst generally conducting themselves with decorum, every few days they're prone to careering about the place in a demented fury. My landlord believes this is a result of their sex life – principally the fact they don't have one. Quite.

And this erratic behaviour extends to their eating habits. Some days they scoff till their eyes fall out, whilst on others they seem perfectly content to lapse into a determined diet. Scarface 2 is the worst. He doesn't appear to have eaten for the past two days and I'm concerned he might faint in the courtyard or start hallucinating. If he doesn't liven up soon I'll have a person-to-pussy talk with him. And if that doesn't work I'll fill the vacuum cleaner with Pussy-Bics, shove the hose down his throat and switch on in reverse mode. That should resolve the problem. (Only joking, cat lovers.)

Scarface 1 is the more phlegmatic of the pair refusing, as all true cats should, to allow anything to affect its routine or dignity. Yesterday he inadvertently nose-dived into a full water tank in the courtyard. There was an almighty commotion for about thirty seconds and water flew in all directions. But he still contrived to clamber out dry.

And now the goats. My problems in this respect have increased during the past week by a third as there are now four of them. From precisely where this interloper appeared I haven't the first idea. Maybe it just came visiting, then liked it and stayed. Damned audacity.

I don't intend dwelling on them for long but some things need to be said. They have the combined intelligence of a pound of carrots and smell appalling. I've seen flies drop from the sky as they stroll past. And how Mr Al-Khalifi believes them to be no trouble is utterly beyond me. The guy next door thinks they're all hooligans. I agree with the guy next door.

I've named them Arsenal, For, The, and Cup. It seemed a splendid notion to open my front door each day at feeding time and shout 'Arsenal For The Cup' at the top of my voice. Unfortunately all four of the buggers are rarely to be seen together and just bawling 'For, The' somehow fails to engender the same satisfaction.

Leaving for work on Saturday, I discovered they'd devoured both of my car wing mirrors. Not that you'd have guessed from their faces. I could all but see a bubble floating innocently above their heads claiming 'It wasn't our fault'. I was furious. Showing them the car-hire company's invoice, I enquired if they considered it reasonable I should slave all day to afford a hired car, only for them to eat it. They gazed back at me like I was selling raffle tickets. I then forbade them from going near the car again without permission. Mind you, I don't intend to give them permission. Of course it's early days, but it wouldn't surprise me to discover during the coming months that keeping goats has no redeeming features. And I don't anticipate many visitors.

Relating all this to colleagues when phoning my London office at lunchtime, their lack of interest surprised me.

'Guess what,' I said, 'the goats have eaten my car,' exaggerating just a touch. And what did I get back?

'Fancy that. Aren't all these roadworks on the M25 a disgrace?'

After this car episode and my subsequent protestations,

IF THE SUN DOESN'T KILL YOU,

Mr Al-Khalifi suggested it was probably a cry for help which, in the long term, could be resolved by showing them lashings of affection supplemented with repetitive training. Again the guy next door disagreed. He suggested repetitive bashing over the head with a metal shovel could be more productive. Once again, I side with my neighbour. Perhaps I'll try leaving their food in the middle of the Doha ring road. (Only joking, goat lovers. Goat lovers?)

As a final throw of the dice, to use a singularly maddening expression, if things don't improve, maybe I'll inaugurate a Qatar branch of Goats Anonymous. There must be others enduring all this nonsense. We could have our own tie.

If I ever compile a list of things best avoided for the rest of my life, goats will definitely be on it. Along with table tennis tournaments, high-sided vehicles and Nina Myskow. Sorry. I must go. I can hear a disturbance outside.

3
To L and back.

Do you know which country has a driving test which consists of steering in reverse for thirty minutes around an obstacle course in the police stadium, at six o'clock in the morning in front of barracking spectators?

Do you know which country has a driving test which has a failure rate of eighty-two per cent?

Do you know which country ensures all its visitors must take its driving test by refusing to recognise an international driving licence?

If you've answered Qatar to each of these questions you're beginning to catch on. For if anything symbolises life here, it's the driving test. And I take mine tomorrow.

It's three weeks since I arrived here and this infamous ordeal has increasingly dominated my time during the past ten days. Regulations only allow it to be taken in a manual car and having previously always driven automatics in Britain, a short familiarisation course in a geared car has been necessary at the local state-run driving school. Or at least it was intended to be short.

The confrontation with the gears and clutch I found more

problematical than expected, a situation not enhanced by my instructor's inability to speak a word of English. During the first lesson, I managed forward progress only in a series of five-yard lurches before stalling the engine. This soon resulted in the man refusing to remain with me in the car as I apparently made him feel sick. Instead he watched from outside, no great inconvenience as during the entire lesson I failed to drive out of eyesight.

Soon finding it easier to teach myself, after six sessions in as many days, I felt sufficiently confident to book the test. The first part, which comprised the medical and oral, was completed today. Tomorrow it's the actual driving test in the stadium and if this morning's proceedings were remotely indicative then I'm in for a curious encounter.

I reported to the police medical centre at seven o'clock, accompanied by Vincent, my driver during the past three weeks. He's been required as it's forbidden for anyone who hasn't passed the test to drive on public roads in Qatar – a measure designed to ensure the highest possible motoring standards throughout the country. (I'm saying nothing.)

Vincent is an intriguing character. He's thirty-five years old, built like a block of flats and his thick, inverted moustache gives him the appearance of an old-time pirate. I'd never met anyone who looks as alarming as their passport photograph. Until I met Vincent. Exasperatingly, his ability to speak English is greater than his capacity to understand it, and whilst he can chatter away to me quite reasonably for about ten minutes, should I be injudicious enough to say,

'Hello, Vincent,' he gawps blankly back at me and replies,

'Huh?'

Maybe it's me.

Each morning when entering the car, he insists on saying a prayer before he'll even consider starting the engine. On the first occasion this happened, I must have looked at him with surprise.

'It's prayers for safe journey, Mr Peter. One for you and one for me.'

'OK, so long as I'm included.'

We've had no accidents so it must have worked. And believe me, that's no bad record for three weeks on Qatari roads.

I got on well with Vincent and was even invited to his home for a meal. The food was good, but it was somewhat of an ordeal as, in keeping with their cultural custom, my hosts refused to start eating their dinners before I'd made substantial inroads into mine. So there was I tucking into fried chicken, rice and *petits pois*, whilst Vincent, his missus, three kids, her grandmother and the cat, were all sitting watching me. Most embarrassing it was. I won't go again.

Regrettably, during the past few days our relationship has become slightly strained. My working hours are longer than he prefers and we've reached a situation where he won't even start work each morning without reading me his rights under the Geneva Convention. And he will insist on playing his ethnic cassette tapes in the car which, to my ears, sound even worse than a dentist's drill. Perhaps I'll give him a belting of the new Guns and Roses album. That should make a point. But back to the medical centre this morning.

Reporting along with sixty other sacrificial lambs who were to undergo this two-part ordeal, I found myself the lone representative of Europe. We were drawn into groups based on alphabetical order and with the surname of Wood, I'm accustomed to being one of the last into action in such situations. It was the same at school. Always last into the playground. However, as names here are reversed, I hoped being dumped in the P group would considerably reduce the wait. Unfortunately, with ninety per cent of my fellow-victims being called either Abdulla, Ibrahim or Mohammed, my promotion seven letters up the ladder proved noticeably ineffective.

The first event on the agenda was the eye test. I was directed to the medical room which had a deceptively high step at its entrance, one that certainly deceived me and I entered the room by sprawling headlong on the floor. The medical officer was sitting behind an impressive oak desk with a baton tucked under his arm. Peering over his glasses, he looked down at me as if I'd been sick on his trousers. What a misery. If he ever became an undertaker, people would stop dying.

'Yes, can I help you?' he bellowed.

I looked up at him, embarrassed at my subservient arrival.

'I've come to take the eye test.'

'Really,' he said, frowning severely. 'Not a very good start, is it?'

Half an hour later it was on to the police interview room where the oral test to identify road signs was held – a seemingly pointless exercise as if there's one thing that's completely ignored in Qatar, it's the road signs. Actually there are quite a number of things completely ignored in Qatar. But one subject at a time.

I was directed to an officer sitting at a glass-fronted counter on which were stacked about twenty well-worn cards, each depicting a different sign. Around 350 million people in the world speak English. Intuition suggested this man was unlikely to be one of them. But I was counting on that.

We looked at each other through our respective sides of the partition, like visiting time at Dartmoor. The butt of his revolver glinted in sunlight which lasered through the window. Irrespective of age, all policemen in Qatar carry guns. After London this concerns me. So many of them, even in their elegant uniforms, look suspiciously around the age of twelve. And they're the officers.

'Engleesh?'

'Oh, yes.'

He held up a card.

'You know this?'

I looked at it and it was upside down.

'Yes,' I said, and smiled.

Staring suspiciously back at me he returned the card to the pile. A second soon followed.

'OK, you know this?'

Looking intently at the card and then at the policeman, once again I replied,

'Yes.'

He blinked back at me doubtfully – and then had a third go.

'OK,' he said, displaying once more the card he'd started with which was still upside down, 'you know this?'

'Yes,' I quickly replied, sticking purposefully to a winning formula.

Thinking for a moment, the officer then looked across at me and said,

'OK, pass, go.'

And that was it. I'd only said yes three times.

And tomorrow it's on to the stadium and the dreaded confrontation with the obstacle course. If fortune lingers for just twenty-four more hours it's 'So long Vincent.' And no bad thing. On the first day we encountered each other he was suffering from a cold and three weeks later he's still spluttering all over me. But realistically, such hopes may prove a touch optimistic and intuition cautions tomorrow could bring some unexpected developments.

I think I'll go to bed early tonight.

I passed the driving test. Or at least I think I did. So how can I describe it? Chaotic? Yes. Confusing? Certainly. An aid to safer driving? You must be joking!

As instructed, I arrived at the police stadium with Vincent at five o'clock this morning and all participants were commanded to form a queue in alphabetical order. This took us to six o'clock. Then the fun started. For the next four hours, I witnessed an unfolding scene of carnage, performed to the incessant din of crashing obstacles, jeering spectators, and policemen's whistles.

Inside the stadium, two identical courses had been constructed. Each comprised three different obstacles, so a total of six drivers were under test simultaneously. To supervise proceedings a policeman was allocated to each obstacle. He would signify if you'd failed by frantically blowing his whistle at you, and signify if you'd passed by frantically blowing his whistle at you. He would also signify all other instructions, as well as his tea break, by frantically blowing his whistle at you.

Eventually it was my turn. With two other Ps, two Qs and an R, I was called to the rear of the stadium where the cars which were provided awaited us. A breakers' yard came to mind.

It was now almost ten o'clock and the shade temperature was 122° Fahrenheit. No kidding. I can bake egg custard at that heat. There was no shade, of course. And heaven knows what the heat would be inside the non-air conditioned cars. The six of us glanced apprehensively at each other in a desperate search for communal solace, a single spirit in our moment of destiny.

Obstacles to right of them, obstacles to left of them, obstacles in front of them. Into the stadium of death rode the six kindred.

I was second in line of vehicles waiting to enter the stadium, behind a young Filipino I'd noticed looking nervous during the eye test yesterday and looking positively terrified now. He was meant to have parked with his wheels behind a white line at the stadium entrance whilst awaiting instructions to enter, but he'd stopped just too far forward. Noticing this, the policeman in charge of the white line immediately blew his whistle at the poor guy and waved at him to pull back. This he did, reversing straight into me with a bang. Unfortunately, although in neutral, I'd failed to apply the handbrake and immediately ricocheted into the car behind. As its handbrake was on – there's always a smart-ass – this caused me to rebound like a pinball and whack the rear of the Filipino. So the three of us had managed a triple collision before we'd started. No wonder these cars were wrecks, it was us that was wrecking them. Then with impeccable timing the policeman blew his whistle and waved furiously at the guy in front to begin.

The first obstacle required the driver to reverse through two rows of hinged, metal posts placed in an S shape. The gap between each row looked marginally less than the width of the car. Each post fell with a clatter at the slightest contact, which resulted in failure of the test. The starting point was reached by entering at the finish and driving forwards.

The Filipino moved slowly towards the two rows of posts on his way in – and hit the first one he reached. The policeman in charge of the obstacle blew his whistle. The crowd of about three hundred people cheered. The poor guy's driving test had lasted ten seconds. Now it was my turn.

Oozing perspiration, I blinked out from my mobile microwave, and with the steering-wheel held in a blood-draining grip, drove circumspectly through to the start. So far so good.

As I began to reverse, there was a crash from across the stadium which must have placed Baghdad on red alert. Two of the other cars had collided head-on. The policeman in charge of my obstacle promptly dashed to the scene to assist in unravelling the confusion and whilst distracted I took the opportunity to reverse at a considerably more measured pace than is officially allowed, through to the finish. As I emerged unscathed the officer returned. And looked surprised.

'OK, go,' he said, blowing his whistle and pointing to my next destination.

This was a steep ramp about the height of a double-decker bus. The object was to reverse halfway up between hinged posts, stop, drive back down, reverse up again, this time to the top, then negotiate a right angle bend before the ramp levels off. At which point you stop. Got it? As the ramp also abruptly ended at this point, failure to stop would ensure a return to ground level by a quicker and conspicuously more direct route than that by which you arrived.

As I approached the start, another driver had prepared

for his ascent and was already waiting in the reverse position. I could see the fear in his eyes.

He completed the first part with commendable efficiency, reversing halfway, returning to ground level and then getting to the top. At which point his luck ran out. Slowly manoeuvring around the right angle bend, he gently touched one of the posts which clattered to the ramp. The crowd cheered. The policeman blew his whistle. He'd failed.

Sadly, the driver's disappointment at this turn of events must have caused him to panic. Instead of applying the footbrake to stop the car before descending the ramp, he obviously hit the accelerator and shot backwards about six feet before shuddering to a halt with his rear wheels hanging in mid-air over the edge. There was a moment of total silence – then all hell broke loose.

From all directions, whistle-blowing policemen appeared. Five clung grimly to the front of the car, their attempts at preventing it from plunging groundwards not assisted by the driver who preferred to get out. And who could blame him? It was only his weight which was anchoring the vehicle to the ramp, but such technicalities were evidently not his immediate concern. Just self-preservation. The police thought otherwise. Their precious car was at risk and facing an indeterminate future. What a farce.

It was ten minutes before relative calm was restored. The car was driven from the ramp by a policeman, and the last I saw of its previous occupant, he was being escorted to the cells by practically the entire Qatari police force. And now it was my turn. Talk about after the Lord Mayor's Show.

But I was lucky. No sooner had I reversed halfway up the ramp, than the policeman, presumably confused or brassed-off by the morning's events, blew his whistle and waved me away.

'OK, go,' he said, and indicated I should proceed to the last obstacle. Two down and one to go.

The final hurdle was a parking bay comprised of the collapsible posts, into which the car must be reversed, a formidable task with the bay barely of sufficient size to accommodate a bicycle. Or so it seemed.

Moving slowly backwards, I was halfway into the bay when I gently touched two of the posts and watched horrified in my wing mirror as they simultaneously began to fall. As the tears welled inside me, the policeman lifted the whistle swiftly to his lips in anticipation. The crowd took a deep, expectant breath. But wait. All was not lost. The posts, presumably placed too closely, struck each other on their way down and miraculously balanced together at an angle of forty-five degrees, like the tip of an arrow. For a few seconds they shuddered. The policeman hesitated, willing them to fall. The crowd laughed, aiming rubbish to persuade them to fall. But they didn't. And the officer slowly withdrew the whistle, disappointment clouding his face.

So I'd done it. I'd completed the obstacle course. The posts hadn't fallen, and in Qatar we all abide by the official rules. As it transpired, I comprised fifty per cent of the successful candidates this morning. The other fifty per cent was an off-duty policeman.

It's difficult to imagine how anyone got round to inventing a driving test like this. Vincent told me that according to reports on the radio this morning, Gorbachev was deposed yesterday and tanks have reached the outskirts of Moscow. I bet they don't storm it in reverse.

And now it was on to the adjacent police station where anyone completing the course, unless you're an off-duty policeman, is required to undergo one final nightmare. Namely drive a police car, together with two officers, around the streets of Doha. Yesterday, two candidates had been successful in the stadium – a Pakistani and a Thai. They'd been brought back and the three of us, together with the officers, climbed uneasily into the vehicle.

The Pakistani was first behind the wheel and received instructions to drive straight ahead. This he did without mishap for around 200 yards. Then one of the officers instructed,

'OK. Stop. Pass. Go,' and ushered him from the car for an unexpected trudge back to the stadium.

The Thai came next. And with an identical conclusion – 200 yards and out.

Now it was my turn. I awaited my instructions to drive forward for 200 yards before winding up with a 600 yards plod back to the stadium to collect Vincent and the car. Some hope.

For the next five minutes the instructions from the officer beside me flowed continually.

'OK. Forward.' 500 yards.

'OK. Left.' 800 yards.

'OK. Right.' 250 yards.

'OK. Left.' 400 yards.

'OK. Right.' 100 yards.

'OK. Stop.'

We were outside the police canteen. And an alarming thought hit me. Surely they're not going to . . .

'OK. Pass. Go.'

In an instant I was ditched at the roadside, the police car vanishing to the rear of the canteen. Any elation at this successful completion of the driving test promptly evaporated. What a nerve. With no clue as to my location, I began retracing the route, dreading the thought of the mile and a half trek ahead, the unremitting sun indifferent to my misfortune. Call me Mr Ungrateful, but this was a bit thick.

About 300 yards along the road, one of Qatar's dazzling orange and white taxis appeared and responding to my insistent wave, stopped with a screech of whatever brakes it possessed. As any traveller will confirm, it's difficult to encounter a taxi driver anywhere in the world who can't understand at least a few essential words of English. But I found one. In fact I found nine, as during the following fifteen minutes half the taxi drivers in Doha materialised and communally endeavoured to make head or tail of my destination. Eventually, I made it back to the stadium by taxi. The driver didn't understand English but was terrific at charades.

And so it was on to the final, simple formality of collecting my precious new licence. Some hope!

Having been handed a printed form on to which my name, address, employer and passport details were written in Arabic, I was instructed to take it to the Licensing Department tomorrow when I'd be issued with the actual driving licence.

In my office this afternoon, I proudly showed the form to a Sudanese colleague who understood Arabic.

'Very good,' he said, 'but it's not yours. The name on the form is Mohammed Kiam, a Kuwaiti who works for the Refuse Department.'

Oh, dear.

I telephoned the police station to outline the circumstances and was told to return immediately.

The reception area was empty when I entered. On the counter was a push-button wired to an impressive ship's bell screwed to the far wall. Gummed to the button was a printed sign which looked important. But it was in Arabic. I pressed anyway and was instantly deafened by a prodigious clang which reverberated around the room. The bell then plummeted from the wall, hitting the floor with an intensity which would have caused me consternation had I not already lost all hearing three seconds earlier. The officer hurtled in. I watched his lips.

'Why you not read sign?' he bawled, pointing to the button. 'It say press soft.'

Doubtless he realised Arabic was meaningless to me.

'This now big mend cost,' he lamented, executing a temporary repair before scrambling gingerly on to a chair to restore the bell to its original location. 'Please give gift to our charity.'

Being well aware which side my chapatti was buttered, I parted with a modest donation and putting the licence form on the counter, explained that due to an unfortunate mistake I'd been given one belonging to somebody else.

'OK,' said the officer, 'take a seat, have a cup of tea.'

Searching through thousands of forms in an enormous cabinet which could well have contained Kuwait, a few minutes later he pulled out a copy of the document I'd previously given him.

'Yes. Definitely your form. Just a few wrong details.'

'But how can it be my form, there's nothing on it that's correct? It's the wrong name, the wrong address, the wrong employer and the wrong passport details. It's obvious I've got someone else's form and there's someone walking around with mine.'

'No, no,' he insisted, 'definitely your form. Just all the wrong details.'

It was pointless arguing. He might make me retake the driving test. And there would be as much chance of passing it a second time, as there was this licence form was mine.

On leaving the police station, another customer passed me in the doorway and I watched as he approached the counter which was again unattended. After a glance at the sign and a moment's thought, he gave the push-button a vigorous prod – and no need for a deerstalker and magnifying glass to guess what happened next. As the din subsided, the officer dashed in.

'Why you not read sign?' he roared. 'It say press gentle. Please give gift to our charity. This now big mend cost.'

I bet.

26

4
What do you think of it so far?

At three o'clock this morning, I awoke abruptly after a dream which caused me such distress it was impossible to nod off again. I dreamt I'd upset John Major. Heaven knows what I'll say if I ever bump into him. Such a pity. A decent night's sleep would have been welcome following yesterday's exertions at the stadium.

Deceptively, today began well with the euphoria of the driving test coup intensified by news of the birth of a little girl named Rebecca.

Brian and Marie, two perennial friends of mine in London, have become parents for the first time and on hearing this I planned to send them a card of congratulations. Some hope.

Question. What's the connection between buying a greetings card in Qatar and queuing for the check-out at my local Asda in London? Answer. After a slow start things rapidly deteriorate.

Umm Said has been my location today, the first without Vincent. I'll miss his prayers. With just a single street of shops, the town services a few thousand residents, the majority of whom work within the nearby petro-chemical and industrial area. And more of that later.

IF THE SUN DOESN'T KILL YOU,

The only card shop is a tiny place the shape of a lighthouse. Due to its size, none of the cards are actually on display, but are packed neatly away in hundreds of cardboard boxes, none of which give any indication as to the precise nature of their contents. The majority of boxes are kept in a dingy attic immediately above the shop. Access to this is by way of a rusty metal ladder secured to the wall by a single screw and mounted at an angle which can range from 180 to 200 degrees depending on the prevailing climatic conditions. Judicious caution is advised when attempting to scale this menace, or you could end up in a place even higher than the attic. Fortunately, in deference to his customers, it's the practice of the shop's intrepid proprietor to risk his own life to decide which card you intend to buy.

As I entered the shop, he was sitting contentedly beside the door attempting to drink from a huge, metal cup of congealed tea. It looked disgusting. But no worse than his vermilion and bottle-green shirt.

'Hello,' he said. 'Take a seat, have a cup of tea.'

Remaining decisively anchored to the only chair in the shop, he then enquired,

'You like buy card?'

Suspecting he'd all but reached the limit of his English vocabulary, and with myself fluent in approximately one language, a potentially lengthy encounter seemed likely.

'Yes, I want card for new baby, please.'

'New baby. Yes. I go upstairs.'

Having furiously ransacked his desk for a torch, he mumbled a brief prayer before disappearing uncertainly up the ladder into the unlit attic, the torch gripped tightly between his teeth. Five seconds later there was a crash. The torch fell through the attic hatchway and bounced sedately back down the ladder, pursued closely by a set of false teeth.

For the next five minutes, the commotion emanating from above indicated a vigorous search was underway, and one the man was evidently getting his gums into. He then

28

re-emerged, although in a dishevelled condition and with blood trickling from a small laceration which had mysteriously appeared on the bridge of his nose. Clutched in his hand was a card which looked attractive and well-printed. 'Good luck', it read, 'in your new job.'

'No, no, no,' I said, 'this is no good. I want card for new baby.'

The proprietor stared blankly back at me.

'New baby,' he echoed, and then smiled broadly as he got the picture.

'Ah, baby. OK, wait.'

Retrieving his teeth from the floor, he rubbed them ferociously on his shirt sleeve before ramming them into his mouth. He then vanished once again up the mercurial ladder.

Minutes later he reappeared, preceded by a large shower of dust.

'Good?' he enquired hopefully, thrusting a card at me.

'Congratulations', it read, 'on passing your driving test.'

'Driving test,' I said, 'why driving test? It's card for new baby I want. What's driving test got to do with it?'

Of course I could have bought it for myself.

The proprietor appeared suitably crestfallen and quickly shinned once more up the ladder to the attic where he made loud looking noises for the next five minutes. Returning breathlessly and with an air of triumph, he held out a card which I could immediately see had a picture of a baby on the front. Thank goodness for that, I thought.

'Congratulations', the card read, 'on becoming a grandmother.'

A grandmother? By now I wished I'd never heard of Brian and Marie, let alone their new baby. In a world which has given us space travel, heart transplants and toothpaste with added fluoride, a simple greetings card eluded me.

'You're a total cretin,' I bawled, 'and I intend to kill you.'

Actually, what I really said was, 'I'm awfully sorry, but I

need card for new baby. Not grandmother, or new job, or driving test – a new baby.'

The poor man looked back at me, obviously mystified all his efforts weren't being appreciated, and he began to look quite hurt. In desperation, I launched into a selection of gurgling noises to assist him, cradling my arms and rocking them back and forth as if holding a baby.

'Ah, new baby,' he said, as my exertions bore fruit and a sudden realisation loomed up on his face. Thank heavens he's got it at last, I thought, as the proprietor disappeared once again into the attic.

He soon returned beaming with anticipation. On his forehead were beads of perspiration which he wiped with an extravagant gesture on his shirt sleeve before offering me a card. And he'd finally got it right. There was a lovely picture of a cradle on the front.

'Congratulations,' it read, 'on having twins.'

I gave up. The man looked so pleased I hadn't the heart to disillusion him.

Within the next few days, Brian and Marie will receive a card of congratulations on the arrival of their twins called Rebecca. And that's the reason why. Incidentally, don't be too surprised if I end up sending out Mother's Day cards this Christmas.

✳ ✳ ✳ ✳ ✳

Just once in a lifetime, one discovers a place so remarkably stunning one gasps in sheer admiration at the creation of such beauty. A place where some indefinable magical quality transforms the mundane into an extraordinary visual experience. A place which will everlastingly endure as an awesome and unique milestone of man's achievement. A place one could justifiably call a true paradise on earth. The petro-chemical and industrial area of Umm Said is not such a place.

Situated 40 miles south of Doha and approached by road

through the desert, it's about 60 square miles in size and has a high security status which restricts entry to permit holders only. It's controlled assiduously by armed police and seems full of people with an evident preference to be somewhere else. And I'm not surprised. Surrounded on three sides by a forbidding barbed wire fence – the sea taking care of the fourth – Umm Said is home to the processing plant for the country's North Field Gas Project. And it's why I'm in Qatar.

The North Field gas reservoir contains an estimated 510 trillion cubic feet of natural gas deposits making it the largest in the world. It will establish the State of Qatar as a major producer of gas far into the twenty-first century, although some independent estimates already project reserves sufficient for 500 years. First discovered in 1971, it took ten years of exploratory drilling before its vast potential was fully appreciated.

A few statistics. Situated 50 miles offshore, the field extends across an area similar to that of Lancashire, in water depth averaging 150 feet. The gas is trapped in four reservoirs 2 miles below the surface. The construction of the offshore wells and production complex, together with associated onshore processing plants, began in 1988. It became the largest engineering project of its kind in the Middle East during the past decade, employing 5,500 men at its peak and costing $1.5 billion. Impressive eh? Which is where I come in.

The quarter million tons of materials and components required to drag a project of this significance into production – from 500 miles of steel pipeline, to sophisticated computer equipment; from the 700 tons of explosives for blasting the rocky terrain, to individual offshore platforms weighing 500 tons – all are manufactured in factories around the world, principally Britain, France, Italy, Japan and the United States. But having them scattered around the globe is of little use to Qatar. Transportation is required by land, air and, predominantly, sea, and for the past three years since 1988, my responsibility has been to co-ordinate this convergence into either Umm Said seaport or Doha airport, working from the London office of the venture responsible for these affairs. Anyone still up?

For its second phase, this operation has transferred to Qatar and my time is primarily expended in shuffling each day between Doha, Umm Said and back again to ensure at least some pretence of organisation. Consequently, should you require a barge, helicopter, floating crane, truck or ship, then I'm your man. Providing there's nothing decent on television, of course.

However, as best I recall prior to becoming abruptly dull, I was in the process of extolling the delights of Umm Said. On its northern outskirts is a roundabout which has witnessed some curious events during the past forty-eight hours.

When approaching this roundabout from Doha, there are three available choices – turn right, turn left, or purchase a newspaper, as it's home to a small army of vendors flogging daily papers, pre-eminent amongst which is *The Gulf Times*. Most people buy their newspapers at roundabouts and how these lads cheat death a few hundred times a day whilst dodging between traffic moving in a multiplicity of directions, is an abiding puzzle. Like how hailstones were described before golf balls came along. Being an avid reader of newspapers, I find myself fascinated by *The Gulf Times*. But does it warrant such devotion from its eager band of salesmen? I think maybe it does.

I believe a free press is fundamental if we are to attain the quintessential standards we should all expect from a democratic society. Mind you, I also believe in trains running on time, and helping old ladies across the road. *The Gulf Times*, sadly, does not yet qualify to march behind the free press banner, as together with the remaining media in this country, it must ensure its opinions coincide fairly accurately with those of the Al-Thani family – or as it's known in Qatar – the Government.

THE WASHING MACHINE WILL

Printed daily in glorious black and white, it's the only English language newspaper published here and concentrates on reporting news principally from Arab, African and Asian countries, using a purely factual format which avoids either undue conjecture or unnecessary levity. Let's be honest, it's bloody boring. However it's this very rigid presentation of the news which makes the paper such riveting reading, with many stories which would seem mildly amusing if reported in British newspapers, becoming quite delightful when delivered with *Gulf Times* sobriety.

I have four characteristic examples from today's edition which I quote verbatim and will be incorporated into my *Gems from The Gulf Times* scrapbook already into its second volume.

The first extract is the concluding section of an extremely tedious report by The Acting Commissioner of Police in Sudan, concerning an incident which took place in the desert town of El-Obeid. I trust the translation into English from its original Arabic hasn't occasioned any embellishment of the details.

Matters got definitely out of hand in El-Obeid when a soldier tried to rob an old woman. My local police captain reported that one of his officers endeavoured to stop the soldier from stealing the old woman's washing.

This annoyed the soldier who shot both the officer and the old woman. Then another officer who was passing shot the soldier and four other soldiers who tried to come to his rescue.

By this time tempers were getting badly frayed. The army sent in a platoon and shot seven policemen. The police were then joined by a group of Zambian wild-life experts who shot most of the soldiers and drove the remainder away. Several Zambians were also shot.

At this point I myself arrived and was shot, along with my driver. No one is sure by who but when I have recovered there will be a full investigation into the whole matter.

The second extract comes from the Asian section of the paper and is headed Kabul, Afghanistan.

> A senior Afghan colonel visited Paris, France, at the weekend on a secret defence procurement mission, military sources said yesterday. He bought twenty-two donkeys for the Army's Mounted Regiment. The animals, eleven males and eleven females, were supplied by a company who said they were under strict orders to divulge nothing about the deal struck at a farm near Paris.
> ['*Psst. 'Ello there. Anyone want any donkeys?*']

Now an unfortunate report from Syria.

> Damascus housewife, Nabilla Sultan, broken hearted at her husband's threatened desertion of her, jumped from her third floor apartment block in a suicide attempt. She landed on her husband, Ali Sultan, who was walking along the street. He was killed but she survived.

Had it been reported anywhere but in *The Gulf Times*, I'd be a touch sceptical about that one.

To conclude, the following report is an extreme example of the attitude to women which prevails to varying degrees in the Muslim societies of the Middle and Far East. The Islamic philosophy has many aspects to commend it. Its debasing of women is not one of them. Muslims, of course, do not accept this Western perception that Islam treats women as inferior. They claim to believe the opposite. You pays your money . . .

> A tribesman in the Indonesian province of Irian Jaja who killed his wife with a bottle was ordered to give away 11 cows as a symbol of regret, the daily newspaper Kompas said.

THE WASHING MACHINE WILL

The newspaper said the penalty was ordered by a meeting of villagers which also asked the unidentified man to bury his wife in the couple's house.

'This is to remind people passing by the house not to repeat the same crime,' Tabangkwari village chief Ibub Beno was quoted as saying.

And back now to the curious events at the Umm Said roundabout – and who knows, this could yet build into something interesting. You'll recall this offers the choice to turn right, leading to the industrial and residential areas, or left, which extends your journey through the desert for a further 2 miles before the road abruptly ends – in even more desert.

On Tuesday, I was approaching this roundabout on my daily journey between Doha and Umm Said, when I observed a small army of Filipinos (or was it an army of small Filipinos?) who were working impressively in the heat to erect the structural support for an enormous road sign.

Some hours later, I again passed the spot and this time the complete sign had been erected, although its face had been covered with sacking, its crucial message still to be revealed to an eagerly awaiting public.

The following morning, after a sleepless night during which I could barely restrain my excitement as to the information this sign would convey, I once again approached the roundabout. And there in full splendour was the sign, now unmasked, which read in Arabic and English, 'Rubbish Tip' and there was a large arrow pointing to the right. The arrow, of course, was only in English.

This information surprised me as I'd never seen a rubbish tip on that particular road, albeit differentiating between a rubbish tip and the rest of Umm Said is tougher than you might suppose. Turning right as usual, I looked for evidence of this tip as I continued through to the industrial site. But saw nothing.

That evening, circumnavigating this same roundabout on my return to Doha, I observed the sign had once more been covered with sacking. This show could run forever.

Approaching the spot this morning, my attention was drawn to a group of the previously mentioned Filipinos who were gathered expectantly around the sign. Stopping the car some 50 yards away, I watched as one of their number clambered adroitly upwards and removed the sacking with a single, deft tug. And what do you know? It still read, 'Rubbish Tip' in both Arabic and, of course, English, but this time the arrow was pointing in the opposite direction – to the left.

With its location now categorically established, and to appease my aroused curiosity, I decided to turn left to see what a Qatari rubbish tip looked like. I drove for about 2 miles and then, as previously, the road came to an abrupt end with no evidence of a tip. There was, however, a second new sign. 'Rubbish Tip' it read. And the arrow? It pointed back along the road towards the original source of the confusion.

I hope you wanted to know all that.

5
Bring back Michael Fish.

It's 3 September 1991, a date certain to acquire significance in the history of Qatar, as the Emir, His Highness Sheikh Khalifa Bin Hamad Al-Thani, has today inaugurated the North Field Gas Project. Qatar has officially embarked on the first stage of the exploitation of its natural gas resources which will herald the beginning of a new era of development and prosperity. Catapulted into third place in the world league of gas-rich nations behind Iran and whatever we call the Soviet Union at the moment, and with one-eighth of the earth's known gas reserves, an expanding status in global industrial terms seems assured. Discuss.

In honour of this occasion, today was decreed a national holiday and this afternoon the inauguration ceremony was held in an enormous marquee in the desert at Umm Said, attended by an impressive array of dignitaries. Televised live, one hundred guests were invited with the heads and foreign ministers of umpteen countries present, in addition to numerous ambassadors – all emphasising Qatar's new-found eminence. I missed the proceedings on television. I was invited to the ceremony.

*

IF THE SUN DOESN'T KILL YOU,

Being a suit and tie job, I arrived at the marquee in some discomfort with the outside temperature well in excess of 100° Fahrenheit. Security was impressive and anything that moved bristled with modern weaponry. Helicopters, trucks, jeeps, soldiers, cockroaches.

The whirring cameras of Qatar television were already transmitting and whilst endeavouring to seem wonderfully cool for the viewers, I just grew even hotter. And how come the Arabs looked so impossibly comfortable in their dish-dashas? (They're the long white sheets.) Didn't they know it was sweltering?

Next, a brass band showed up to regale us with a selection of tunes we all love. Although not any more. Dressed in full band gear, my discomfort was surely nothing compared to theirs as we remained in the remorseless glare of the sun. After thirty minutes of melodious virtuosity, I concluded this was the most impressive live performance by a brass band I'd ever heard. Naturally it was also the only live perfor-mance by a brass band I'd ever heard. Eventually they blew themselves to a frazzle and all the guests were cordially invited to storm the marquee. At last!

Rows of chairs had been positioned and specifically allocated with name tags. On each chair lay a bound pro-gramme of events printed in both Arabic and English and with a gold tassel hanging from the side. The front row, for high ranking guests, comprised colossal armchairs of a quite sumptuous nature. The second row, reserved for those of slightly lower eminence, was only marginally less opulent. My name was on a stool at the back. No, I'm joking. I was positioned discreetly in the third row on a padded, wooden bench with an optional cushion. Mind you, there were only three rows.

In an attempt to keep us cool, or in my case conscious, a dozen electric fans on stems 10 feet high and with blades 3 feet in diameter, had been connected to a portable gen-erator which droned interminably from the far corner of the marquee. Occasionally it burst into a vibrating frenzy like a departing 747. They barely helped. We were melting like a heap of soggy aspirins.

But relief was at hand. Row one was served tea from traditional gold-plated jugs. With their long, curved spouts and arabesque patterns they looked magnificent, their origins conceivably predating even Judith Chalmers's suntan. Row two received their tea from splendidly ornate cut glass pitchers which were surely worth a fortune. I enjoyed my can of Coke.

The Emir arrived an hour behind schedule. But we all waited. A lengthy speech was followed by a lengthy speech, which was followed by prayers, and then by a lengthy speech. Then it was all over.

Good luck to Qatar with its gas. This has been a significant day for both the state and its people of which they're justifiably proud. If they proceed wisely, as initial indications suggest, the North Field Gas Project will bring prosperity to Qatar for many decades.

✳ ✳ ✳ ✳ ✳

Question. What can be extremely difficult to locate in Qatar? Answer. Qataris. And you think I'm joking?

Having resided here for nearly six weeks, prior to this afternoon's inauguration, I'd come across only one Qatari and that was my landlord. In all, there are only around 120,000 of them, Qataris, I mean, not landlords. This represents little more than a quarter of a population in which men outnumber women by two to one. This imbalance results from the high proportion of male immigrant workers who comprise eighty-five per cent of the actual labour force.

So Qataris are very much a minority in their own country. And with the women rarely seen in public, and the majority of men managing their own businesses or strategically placed in senior positions within the government or other state-related organisations, it's no surprise they're not exactly thronging on every street fraternising with the general *hoi polloi*.

Consequently, Qatar is kept functioning at ground level by immigrants, nationals from the Indian sub-continent comprising half the total population, whilst Europeans amount to around five per cent. English, in one whimsical form or another, represents the unifying language.

For the most part, public services are maintained by itinerants from the Philippines or Thailand, shops and offices staffed by these workers from the Indian sub-continent, and taxis driven by creatures from another planet. Even the army and police have substantial numbers of foreign nationals amongst their non-commissioned ranks.

As a result, my landlord, Mr Abdulla Khulifa Al-Khalifi, is the only Qatari with whom I'm acquainted, and a genuinely affable man he seems. Around forty years old, he speaks perfect English with regard to both grammar and pronunciation and when I commented on this, he explained it was a consequence of his wife coming from Australia. Frankly, I didn't see the connection.

Having returned from the inauguration late this afternoon, at his invitation, I visited the home of Mr Al-Khalifi. There are certain formalities, or courtesies, to be observed when in the company of an Arab and my concentration was primed to ensure no violation of these. Sitting with legs crossed in such a way as to display the sole of the shoe, for example, would be considered an insult, the practice of wearing open sandals without socks in this hot climate establishing the foot as one of the less engaging bodily features to have shoved up your nostrils. Also the Koran, the Islamic bible, decrees food and drink should only be accepted and consumed with the right hand, the left being the one nominated for less hygienic pursuits of a nature we can hastily wipe from our minds.

THE WASHING MACHINE WILL

The purpose of my visit was three-fold. Firstly, having been most impressed at my receiving an invitation to the ceremony, Mr Al-Khalifi had taped the proceedings on his Betamax and insisted I view the whole business once again. On each of the four occasions my wilting figure fleetingly appeared, he took immense delight, giving whoops of joy and pointing excitedly at the screen. Swinging around in his chair, he'd then peer searchingly towards me to ensure no mistake in identification. By the time the programme had dragged to its belated conclusion, I bore the inevitable makings of a star.

Next came the food, and the second reason for my visit. Mr Al-Khalifi had suggested I eat with him.

'My wife will prepare a good Arab meal. Better than your pies and puddings.'

It's not always easy to identify the constituents of a good Arab meal and certainly not acceptable form to enquire. It looked like boiled goats' hoofs. In fact it tasted like boiled goats' hoofs. Mr Al-Khalifi loved it, and even I admit detecting a slight improvement towards the latter stages. Before leaving Qatar, I must learn that whilst eating boiled goats' hoofs may appear to be one of the more unpleasant facts of life – like woolly balaclava helmets – there are more things to savour in the world than eggs, bacon, chips and baked beans. And I was gratified to note that Mrs Al-Khalifi, or Moira as I now call her, sat and ate with us, which wouldn't have occurred had she been a Qatari. Stuck in the kitchen with the cat more like.

The third prong of the evening's socialising involved an excursion with my landlord to an extraordinary concert given by a visiting Albanian dance and accordion group. And how can I describe this concert? Abysmal, I think, would be an appropriate description. So dreadful was it, the latecomers were colliding in the gangways with the people who were creeping out early. So what were we doing there in the first place? You may well ask.

The State of Qatar is not yet a leading performer on the world stage. Like many countries of similar status, it compensates for its walk-on role by engaging in an endless succession of exchange visits between its own dignitaries and those from countries of a comparable ilk. Not a day passes without someone arriving in Doha to inform us all of the astonishing contribution Qatar has made towards the enhancement of world stability and, in turn, to be told what magnificent advances his own country has achieved in the furthering of the democratic processes. It's enough to make you feel sycophantic.

But these exchange visits are not confined to politicians. A regular procession of what *The Gulf Times* calls cultural tours are organised for the delight of we residents. The price of a ticket for one of these shows is usually twenty riyals, about three pounds, although the lack of local enthusiasm for such occasions can generally be assessed when Qatar Radio announces that a quantity of free tickets are available, usually in approximately equal proportion to the capacity of the local theatre.

And that's how Mr Al-Khalifi and I came to be watching this Albanian dance and accordion group. The tickets were free. And other than pray five times a day, and acquire a suntan, there's not a lot else to do in Qatar. So nothing to lose. It was a mistake we won't repeat.

The audience could generously be described as thin on the ground. Most seemed racked with misgivings about the whole affair and ten minutes after the scheduled start an aura of foreboding began drifting around the auditorium. Whatever's the opposite of sitting on the edge of your seat, the audience was certainly doing it. In the nick of time to staunch scattered mutterings of discontent from the floor, a disembodied voice made an incomprehensible announcement and the group swept exultantly on stage to a spontaneous round of silence.

The highpoint of the evening arrived soon after the start

when the spotlight exploded, and during the ensuing confusion the lead accordionist plummeted exquisitely off the
stage. It took five minutes to repair the light and heave the
accordionist back up before a resumption of the performance was possible. For the remainder of the evening the
poor man reluctantly negotiated the stage with a pronounced limp – pronounced limp.

Moments later, and presumably due to this unscheduled
excitement, the group's narrator, whose daunting task it
was to explain to the rest of us what the hell these lunatics
were actually doing, suddenly developed hiccups and
dashed off to the wings to recover. By the time he'd
lurched sheepishly back on the stage, the group members
outnumbered the audience. It's true to say talent such as
this is only seen once in a lifetime. It's a pity it had to be
mine.

Proceedings then reached a crushing climax. In a move
which could only have been brought about by desperation,
the narrator began reciting traditional Albanian poetry to
the amazement of we stalwarts that remained. I wonder if
this man keeps lemmings? The poems were accompanied
by explanatory slides projected from the side of the stage
in the general direction of a blue striped sheet slung haphazardly across the piano.

Sadly, most of the images were illuminating the luckless
lead accordionist. He blinked furiously in response, before
relocating his chair in a more secluded position. This left the
floor and the leg of the piano as the principal recipients of
the projector's aim. But not for long, as a crash from the
wings and an abrupt realigning of the beam to the ceiling
indicated a further unplanned addition to the programme.
Get the car started.

Mr Al-Khalifi and I were last to leave the theatre some
thirty seconds later. We had no regrets. Things had gone
from bad to verse.

According to *The Gulf Times*, another performance of

the show is scheduled for tomorrow evening. Book now to avoid disappointment.

✳ ✳ ✳ ✳ ✳

It rained in Qatar yesterday for the first time in a year. No, rained perhaps is the wrong word. A tempest of blitzkrieg proportions is probably more accurate. On a scale of 1 to 10, this was a 58. It only lasted twenty-four hours and came more than two months after National Pray For Rain Day. What a difference a pray makes!

I suspected it might happen as yesterday's *Gulf Times* had warned of occasional clouds and a steady breeze. Predicting the unusual is essential in a desert environment, and in this respect nothing is better unqualified than *The Gulf Times*. And there's no excuse. Being a professional weather forecaster in Qatar is not the most demanding occupation known to man. I doubt the duration of the entire meteorological curriculum undertaken by the Weather Bureau's team of highly trained experts extends beyond twenty minutes – or fifteen if there's camel racing on television.

Nevertheless, the Bureau is conspicuously adept at ensuring it's not taken for granted by making the task appear impossibly complex, which it further confuses by granting the whole affair a classified information status. This reluctance to divulge any lowdown on the weather may not be unconnected to the law concerning the maximum temperature in which any of us are allowed to work. This is prescribed as 50°C, that's 122°F when seasonally adjusted, a figure frequently achieved during the summer months. And if left in ignorance as to the true temperature, how can we proletariat determine when to down pick-axes and put our feet up with a refreshing glass of water? How indeed?

As no meteorological information is broadcast on state radio or television, in attempting to establish impending weather in Qatar there are just three practised methods of varying reliability.

Method No. 1
Dial 850111, which is the recorded forecast updated daily and issued in both Arabic and English. That seems simple doesn't it? Unfortunately, the guy reading the information pronounces his words in such a fashion as to render the English version not only unintelligible, but indistinguishable from its Arabic equivalent – or, indeed, the Arabic version indistinguishable from its English equivalent. It's impossible to know which. So count that one out.

Method No. 2
Buy *The Gulf Times* and read their version. This will be one of two alternatives printed on an approximately equal number of occasions throughout the year. Namely, Hot and sunny with occasional heat haze (always a good bet, of course) or, We regret weather unavailable today.

So if daily precision forecasting is your requirement, forget *The Gulf Times*.

Method No. 3
Look out the window. If it's not the one day in the year when Qatar disappears under five feet of torrential rain, it will be dry, hot and sunny, the only variable being the temperature which can range from 'phew what a scorcher' through to 'you must be barmy if you think I'm going out in this heat'.

I declare method No. 3 the winner.

Now where was I? Yesterday's drenching.

It was raining when I awoke and I suspected the downpour had been under way for some hours when I glanced into the courtyard from the bedroom window and saw Arsenal resolutely wading belly-deep through the water, ferrying both cats to dry land on its back. Or something like that. Pulling on some shorts I ventured outside to consider the merits of building an ark.

The courtyard resembled a moat. All five members of Status Quo were huddled in a line on top of a section of the exterior wall, together with a sixth chicken which mysteriously appeared at the villa last week. I've named it Paxo so it fully understands who's the boss around here. As this section of wall is overhung by an old builder's hoist belonging to Mr Al-Khalifi, it offered partial protection from both the deluge above and the torrent below, and indicated that chickens may not be as stupid as I'd previously imagined. However, it was probably the highest point they'd ever reached and all six looked utterly dejected, doubtless considering whether drowning might prove an even better option than vertigo.

But a long-standing mystery was resolved. After weeks of doubt, the schizophrenic enigma on two legs which couldn't decide if it was a chicken or a duck, has finally discovered the truth. It was having a marvellous time splashing around out there. So it's definitely a duck. All it needed was someone to spend a little time giving encouragement and understanding. I wonder who it was?

Leaving the livestock to fend for themselves, I waded out to the car and drove warily into Doha. And there I came upon a new mystery. Where the hell does everyone go in Qatar when it rains? The place was deserted. More than 450,000 people had just disappeared without trace. The only signs of activity were the water trucks, their routine irreversible, as they splashed doggedly through the flood on their daily run to irrigate the palm trees which so stylishly adorn the sea front.

Now accepting that around 100,000 people had probably been lost for ever down the latest range of colossal holes which immediately appeared in the roads, this still left more than 350,000 unaccounted for. The whole area looked like a long abandoned Hollywood film set.

I returned to the villa. The goats were crouching forlornly under the builder's hoist, watching the cats who were sitting disconsolately about halfway up, who were watching the chickens perched grimly on top of the wall. And they were all watching Duck, still splashing happily around in the courtyard, clearly relishing the discovery of its true identity.

So was it the end of civilisation as we know it? Well, actually, no it wasn't. This morning it's as if nothing had happened. The roads of Doha have returned to their accustomed bustling activity, as people pursue their respective trades, or plunge headlong down the latest holes. In quiet corners, clandestine groups have gathered to exchange stories of how they lived through the havoc of the previous twenty-four hours. What did you do the day it rained in Qatar, daddy?

According to the weather column in today's *Gulf Times*, we had eleven hours of sun yesterday with occasional heat haze. Really? Whoever's responsible for issuing this weather information is an idiot. In fact I've just decided what could be done with one of those flaming great holes in the road. Providing the duck's not splashing about in it, of course.

To mitigate my exasperation at the inability of the authorities to introduce even a shred of efficiency into their weather forecasts, I composed a letter of complaint yesterday to *The Gulf Times* Letters Page, an irregular feature as few people are aware of their address. It was only by stalking one of their delivery vans back to its lair last night, that I made the discovery.

To my amazement, and their credit, my letter was printed this morning with an explanatory reply which raises more questions than it answers, and shows they know slightly less than nothing about forthcoming weather.

Dear Sirs,
On 1 October, it rained continuously in Qatar for almost twenty-four hours and yet the weather forecast printed in *The Gulf Times* that day stated, 'hot and sunny with occasional heat haze'.

How was it possible for such a substantial bank of raincloud, which must have covered several thousands of square kilometres across Qatar, Saudi, Bahrain and Kuwait, not to have been foreseen by your weather department?
Yours faithfully,

Ed.
I think you have misunderstood our information. What is printed in our weather section is not the weather expected on the day of issue, but the weather for the previous day.

So now we know. The fact they also printed, hot and sunny with occasional heat haze this morning, was apparently considered irrelevant. Little wonder their daily horoscope is such baloney.

However, as a consequence of this correspondence, shortly after lunchtime today I received a quite unexpected telephone call from the Qatar Weather Bureau. It invited me to visit their office to discover the process by which the forecasts are produced for *The Gulf Times* and also recorded for telephone enquirers to 850111.

Accepting this magnanimous proposal, I visited them this evening, although with some disquiet, recognising the difficulty I'd always experienced with regard to the English pronunciation of the Bureau's recorded representative. And if they all spoke like that...!

48

THE WASHING MACHINE WILL

As it transpired it was an even greater disaster than I'd anticipated. During twenty minutes of explanation, I doubt I understood more than five words spoken by the instructor. This proved something of an embarrassment as he was an expat from Glasgow.

6
Everything takes two weeks. But from when?

'In Sha'Allah' are the two most frequently heard words in Qatar and are normally used by someone immediately following a request for them to undertake a simple task. The literal translation from Arabic is 'God willing', but in reality it means 'Sorry mate, there's not the remotest chance I'll do it, as the minute you've gone I'll either forget all about it, or deliberately delay doing it to make you even more grateful when I do get round to it.'

I first encountered this In Sha'Allah routine soon after my arrival here, when I bought myself a portable cassette player from the local electrical shop. Cheap, pirated cassette tapes are available at a quarter of the price of the genuine article in Britain and whilst the quality could not be described as brilliant, it's reasonable considering the reduced cost.

After using the new cassette player for a few days, it developed a fault which rendered it inoperative. Returning to the shop, I explained the trouble to the assistant.

'No problem. It's got guarantee. We repair.'

'Good. How long take?'

'Two weeks. All repairs two weeks.'

'But I've only had it a few days. Please have ready in one week.'

'In Sha'Allah.'

The following week I returned.

'Sorry, not finish. Please come next week.'

So the repair took its pre-ordained fortnight. First blood to In Sha'Allah.

Two days later the machine developed another fault.

'Hello, back again?' the assistant said cheerfully. 'Take a seat, have a cup of tea. Problem?'

'It's broken again. I've only owned machine three weeks and you've had it for two of them. Please repair quickly. I want to collect tomorrow.'

'In Sha'Allah,' he replied ominously.

It was ready two weeks later and operated correctly for precisely ten minutes before failing for the third time. I stormed back to the shop.

Intuition appeared to have warned the assistant that trouble was imminent and as I entered he was primed for action like a coiled spring.

'Hello, take a . . .'

'Never mind about that. This machine useless. I want replacement.'

Immediately I said the word replacement, I knew I'd introduced a controversial element into the proceedings as the assistant turned green and began shivering like a startled blancmange. Taking the initiative I continued,

'I want to speak to manager. Please get manager now.'

'Manager problem,' he mumbled.

'Why? What problem?'

'Manager not speak English.'

'OK. What nationality is he?'

'Thai.'

'And what nationality are you?'

'Thai.'

'Right, no problem. You translate.'

'Sorry problem.'

'What problem?'

'I don't speak English.'

'What do you mean you don't speak English? What do you think we're speaking now?'

'Oh, understand.'

He beamed with delight and called the manager. Wearing mauve, corduroy, flared trousers, a maroon shirt, a yellow check sports jacket and a pair of flashy gold cuff-links, the manager slid discreetly into the shop from behind a green felt curtain at the rear. There was a knotted handkerchief on his head. He had a face like castor oil and nodded repeatedly like a visiting bishop. Christ! Now I'm not one of those people who thinks that just because a man wears mauve, corduroy, flared trousers, a maroon shirt, a yellow check sports jacket, flashy gold cuff-links and has a knotted handkerchief on his head, it necessarily indicates he's a complete bonehead. But this man was a complete bonehead.

The three-way conversation which ensued can be paraphrased as follows.

'I want a replacement.'

'He wants a replacement.'

'Tell him he can't have one.'

'You can't have one.'

After a heated exchange lasting some minutes during which superficial damage was inflicted on his knotted handkerchief, the manager agreed to a replacement machine and I departed with it still in its box. Carrying it home, it occurred to me that for a cassette player it felt remarkably light.

Back at the villa I inspected the machine. Or what there was of it as astonishingly there was nothing inside. It was a shop display model with a plastic exterior and very little else.

The manager was just locking the shop when I hurtled through the door. The knotted handkerchief had been replaced by a blue and white baseball cap and I noticed his studded, green cowboy boots which had somehow eluded me earlier. They added a subtle hint of sophistication to his appearance. What in heaven's name does this man wear on his day off?

Without speaking, I placed the machine on the counter and opened the back. The manager looked inside, then apprehensively at me before scuttling to the other side of the counter – presumably as a safety precaution. Disappearing through the curtain to the back, he soon returned with another machine.

Unpacking it from its box, he fitting a plug and connected it to an electrical testing circuit beside the counter. Instantly every light and appliance in the shop fused and we were left in near darkness and with a pungent smell of burning. Is this madman related to the guy who installed my cooker? Within seconds he'd produced a torch, two paraffin lamps and an enormous box of fuses. Obviously this diversion occurred more often here than it does in Rumbelows.

Once normality was restored, the manager brought forth yet another machine which he unpacked and tested, this time successfully. After repacking and dropping two bananas into the box, presumably as a placatory gesture, he pushed it towards me with solicitous care. Not a word had been spoken between us since I'd entered the premises some twenty minutes earlier.

As I departed, I noticed a sign hanging on the inside of the door. 'Please visit us again' it read. In Sha'Allah.

Since resolving the difficulties with the cassette player, I've found little time to plough through the selection in the cheap, cassette tape shop as the one-day weekend in Qatar proves barely sufficient for domestic chores. Nevertheless, last Friday, I made a determined effort to get there. For all the good it did me.

The previous evening I'd been listening to a three-hour

programme of rock music which is transmitted each day on the local radio station, as, in addition to its Arabic service, Qatar Radio broadcasts a daily schedule in English, combining sobriety with levity, not always by design. Liable to disappear from the wavelengths at unspecified times, some of the presenters, a mixture of nationalities representing the various non-Arabic speaking residents of Qatar, don't always employ a language which is immediately identifiable as English. And come to think of it, it produces probably the most boring news bulletins of any country in the civilised world. But given that all things are comparative, it's not bad – certainly pre-eminent amongst its counterparts in the Gulf.

Because of work commitments, I'd not previously listened to this evening rock show and was drawn by its presenter whose name, as was indicated on various occasions by a natty jingle, proved to be Tim Manns. It was his professionalism which caught my attention. Equal, or superior, to what I'm accustomed to hearing on Radio 1 or Capital in London, it seemed incongruous in its surroundings. What was someone this competent doing here? Enthused by his selections, apart from the odd rhythm and blues track, I made my long overdue inspection of the cassette tape shop.

And who should I meet there? Tim bloody Manns that's who. I couldn't believe it. Christ, there are over 400,000 of us in Doha. It was his voice I recognised as he requested an obscure Stevie Ray Vaughan tape. No chance.

We had a lengthy chat and it transpired he's employed in Qatar as a surveyor and does two radio shows a week as an extra. Having worked full time for many years on Radio Bahrain both as a DJ and presenter, his broadcasting experience is more extensive than I'd assumed, which doubtless accounts for his being such a dab hand at the game.

Having arranged to meet next week, Tim dashed off to the chicken market leaving me to concentrate my endeavours in establishing which tapes were in stock – the new Eric Clapton perhaps, or the latest Simply Red.

While entering the shop earlier, I'd observed an ornate, multicoloured sign in the window which stated quite simply, and in large letters, 'New Arrivals'. On the inside wall was another of these signs with an arrow pointing downwards to a huge display cabinet. This contained precisely three cassette tapes, one of which was Chubby Checker's *Twisting Favourites Volume 1*, and the other two were *Max Bygraves Christmas Party Time*. Not exactly new arrivals.

It was at this juncture Mr Memnon Menon, the man who owns the shop, dashed in, identifiable from an enormous framed photograph of himself beaming furiously whilst holding a sheet of cardboard across his chest with 'Proprietor – Mr Memnon Menon' printed across it. The picture hung somewhat askew from the wall and although smaller than its subject, the difference was slight.

'Hello,' he panted, 'take a seat, have a cup of tea.'

I thanked him but declined.

'Right,' I said, pointing to the sign. 'I'd like to see the new arrivals, please.'

'Yes, yes,' he replied, smiling anxiously.

'Have you got any?'

'No, no,' he said, looking confused.

Pointing once more to the sign, I slowly repeated, 'I'd like to see the new arrivals, please.'

Suddenly he seemed to appreciate what the hell I was talking about.

'Come back Monday,' he said, giving an enormous smile. He was as short on teeth as he was on cassettes.

The following Monday I returned. The 'New Arrivals' sign was still in the window, and walking to the far end of the shop I discovered there were now only two cassette tapes in the display cabinet. Someone must have bought one of the Max Bygraves.

Mr Memnon Menon was busy screwing a 'Danger

Inflammable Liquid' sign on to the side of his cash register. I didn't ask why.

'New arrivals,' I said, once again indicating towards the sign on the wall. 'Have they come?'

He dropped his screwdriver, presumably in shock at hearing such a ridiculous question.

'No, no. Next week, next week.'

Departing once more, I decided to return some time in the future – like 1998. But not so.

As I passed the shop this morning while heading for the airport to establish their anticipated arrival date for a packet of computer fuses from Houston which I know for a fact landed here six days ago, Mr Memnon Menon spotted me and waved his handkerchief enthusiastically for me to enter.

'New arrivals come,' he grinned.

This surprised me as by now even the display cabinet had disappeared.

Vanishing into a cupboard at the back, he soon re-emerged, this time all but enveloped in a mantle of smiles. And what was he clutching? Of course. Six polythene-wrapped copies of that 'New Arrivals' sign.

Back home at the villa, I decided to cook a tinned mutton and goat pie Mr Al-Khalifi had given me in lieu of a decent washing machine. Placing the tin in the oven, I checked the instructions on the box. Unfortunately these were in Arabic. But so what? Who the hell needs instructions to warm up a meat pie?

Five minutes later there was an explosion from the kitchen. With Arsenal out visiting friends, I was feeding the remaining three goats in the courtyard at the time. It was a surprise evening meal – the surprise being it was those 'New Arrivals' signs.

Heading in some haste for the kitchen, I was matched step for step by the goats. This natural inclination to get involved in other people's business I find immensely irritating. If they can't create their own disorder they hijack someone else's.

When the smoke eventually cleared, I opened the oven door and found my mutton and goat pie had disintegrated into a few thousand pieces which were embedded inside the oven. It was my own fault, of course, as it's obvious I should have made a small hole in the tin before heating the oven. But you just don't think of things like that. Not when you're a busy, international businessman.

Thank God this isn't television.

I was still fanning away remnants of the smoke and spraying the villa with an Egyptian air freshener, when the outside gate bell chimed. It was Mr Al-Khalifi. Surely he hadn't heard the explosion from his car? Smiling gently, his nose twitched slightly in reaction to the exotic whiff of old Cairo.

Making no enquiry as to the origin of the pong, he staggered inside carrying an enormous box containing 500 oranges, apparently surplus to his own requirements. No kidding. Where in heaven's name does someone get 500 oranges? Maybe they fell off the back of a camel.

As a result of this unexpected gift, I achieved a personal milestone, as for only the second time in my life I peeled an orange. It will also be the last.

The task of peeling an orange has always seemed unacceptably messy. Or it was the way I did it. As a result, I've consumed very few in my life, due principally to a dearth of volunteers to perform this odious chore on my behalf. To peel one for your own consumption is tortuous in the extreme, but to tackle it for someone else ... greater love hath no man than this, that a man peels an orange for his friends.

However, being in possession of 500 of the damn things, I decided to risk it. Never again. It took an eight-hour thrashing in the washing machine before my shirt and trousers were fit for public exhibition. And they were part of my summer collection. Anyone fancy 499 oranges?

Mr Al-Khalifi also lent me *The Gulf Times Souvenir Book of the Desert*. It looks interesting. Apparently in the south-west of Qatar towards the Saudi border, is a desert area which has been without rain for seven years and the temperature reaches unimaginable heights during the summer months. Seemingly no one ventures there – although maybe the silly old fool from the Weather Department risked sunstroke to acquire this information. Because that could explain a lot.

Before leaving, my landlord related an Arab joke.

Three nomads were travelling through the desert when they heard a distant cry for help. Following the sound, they came across a man buried up to his neck in the sand.

'Thanks to the Almighty,' said the man. 'I was caught in a sandstorm about an hour ago and can't move. Can you help?'

'Don't worry,' answered one of the nomads, 'we'll dig you out.'

'Praise be,' came the reply, 'but I hope you've brought a shovel as I'm sitting on a camel.'

I think I'll ask Mr Al-Khalifi for a rent reduction.

7
It ain't what you do it's the way that you do it.

During recent weeks, I've developed a friendship with a Qatari who has become a frequent visitor to the villa where we enjoy fascinating discussions concerning our respective cultures and environments. His undemonstrative but loquacious explanation of the Islamic philosophy is absorbing and illustrates its many commendable aspects.

His name is Khaleel and he was one of the small contingent of Qatari troops which helped to liberate Kuwait. He's twenty-seven years old and one of fourteen children from a wealthy and well-educated family. He owns a Mercedes, a BMW and a Range Rover, and has recently insisted on forsaking his traditional dishdasha when visiting me, to parade instead a Union Jack T-shirt I gave him recently to celebrate both his birthday and Britain finishing second in last April's European Song Contest, which for some inexplicable reason was broadcast recently on Radio Bahrain. Three days ago Khaleel shot his eldest brother dead.

I spent half an hour with him in jail today. We didn't discuss his action. Any such questions from me were unnecessary, as I had been fully aware of his intention, method and motive the previous week. I'd urged him to abandon his threat, spending long, intense hours in an attempt to dissuade him. But it was futile. The pride of an Arab is paramount and at times defies reason. And this was one of those times.

When his father died in 1988, Khaleel inherited a substantial amount of money. Last year, Rashid, one of his brothers, asked him for a loan of 700,000 riyals – around £110,000 – as he wished to purchase a house in Dubai. As would be expected within an Arab family, Khaleel readily agreed, withdrew the money from the bank and gave it in cash to Rashid. In Qatar, cheques are only issued between banks. Few companies or individuals will accept them.

Last month Khaleel himself decided to purchase some property and requested the return of his money. Not only did Rashid refuse this request, but rejected any knowledge of the loan. Consequently, Khaleel approached his senior brother, his mother, and then his uncle – the accepted head of the family since the death of his father. All were unsuccessful in their appeals to Rashid who persisted in his denials.

Finally, Khaleel visited the police who advised that being a family matter, they were unable to intercede without evidence. There was none, of course. As Khaleel said, 'You don't ask your own brother for a receipt.'

It was at this juncture he advised the police of his intention to kill Rashid unless the money was returned, or at least the loan acknowledged. The consensus of opinion was that, given the circumstances, the likely judicial consequences of such an act would be between one and two years in jail.

Khaleel contacted Rashid, informing him that unless he conceded receipt of the money by the approaching Friday, he would kill him the following day. He then revisited his uncle, requesting him to formally advise Rashid likewise.

It was at this stage last week that Khaleel first acquainted me with the circumstances. My initial reaction, whilst indicating genuine commiseration for his dilemma, was to suspect exaggeration, a response reinforced when he blithely informed me he was in possession of ten guns, one of which he would use to kill his brother that coming Saturday. My scepticism vanished the following evening when Khaleel, who must have sensed my disbelief, appeared at the villa with a holdall containing the guns, one of them a machine gun. Suddenly this bizarre prospect was a potential reality.

I tried persuasion, I advised caution, I suggested alternatives. But I failed to dissuade him from his declared intention. And it was the absence of anger or passion in his demeanour which convinced me that evening this alarming melodrama could actually happen. Honour was at stake. If the police had indicated he could serve ten years, I doubt it would have influenced his resolve.

Khaleel killed Rashid on Sunday, his only concession to reason being to delay for one day. I cannot understand or justify what he did. There must have been an alternative way to resolve this without leaving a wife and three young children bereaved. They played no part in Rashid's transgression. And the Koran is no advocate of such unilateral behaviour.

My visit to the jail this morning will be the last, my presence being patently unappreciated by the authorities. Arabs prefer to keep their discords to themselves and perceived intrusion is unwelcome. Henceforth our contacts will be confined to letters conveyed through his family.

I'll miss our conversations. And Khaleel's earnest, decorous company. Informed opinion now considers the prophesied one or two years in jail to be over-optimistic. I'm not surprised. My mind recognises such a sentence would be absurd for the magnitude of the crime he's committed. My heart, of course, says otherwise.

I'm told by his mother there's now sufficient evidence to prove the existence of the loan. What a waste.

✳ ✳ ✳ ✳ ✳

The final of the rugby world cup was played at Twickenham today, where Australia beat England, a result which plunged me into a brief period of melancholy. Although a close match, the outcome of which, according to Radio Australia, was in doubt until the final whistle, the Aussies appeared to thoroughly deserve their victory. Bastards. I listened to the commentary of the game at my landlord's place.

You'll recall Moira originates from Australia, and a Melbourne friend of hers called Kylie, yes really, also turned up for the excitement. Kylie, it transpired, is married to a German who works in the Lufthansa office in Doha. In fact, I think he is the Lufthansa office in Doha. I can't pretend I took to her.

'There's good and bad news about Qatar,' she bellowed. I knew what was coming.

'The bad news is it's all sand.' Wait for it . . .

'The good news is there's plenty of it.' Told you.

She has the demeanour of a scrapyard alsatian and would probably have much preferred being at Twickenham scrumming in the front row with her compatriots. Maybe I caught her on a bad day. Somehow I doubt it.

During the broadcast, Moira fed us with a plate of what could only be described as antipodean-inspired rissoles.

'It's amazing what you can do with leftovers,' she proudly announced. I do something better. I throw them away.

Whilst unlikely to have been detected, I admit to harbouring a certain antipathy towards Australians. In fact, I make a point of taking an instant dislike to them. It saves time. This aversion, which extends back to my infant years, is due to one specific and eminently justifiable reason. They usually beat us at cricket. How I recall those sad nights listening to the radio commentaries from Sydney, Melbourne, Adelaide, Brisbane and Perth. And as often as not we got walloped. It never rained in Australia when it was needed.

Following the rugby, I drove to the airport post-office, depositing my vehicle in the car park whilst despatching an accumulation of letters. Gummed on the mail-box was a sign in both Arabic and English, the latter of which instructed, 'Do not put anything inside this post-box unless it will fit inside this post-box'. What a stroke of luck they informed me in time. I had intended putting my vacuum cleaner inside.

Returning to the car, I found it blocked by a pick-up truck which had parked illegally across the exit. It had an ominous air of permanence. Anticipating a prolonged wait, I'd just made myself comfortable in the car when the truck driver returned and following a glance in my direction entered his cab, making no apology for his inconsiderate behaviour. Guessing he could understand English, I remained composed and advised him he'd acted in contravention of the Doha Airport parking regulations of 1988, revised 1990, conduct which rendered his vehicle liable to be removed by the authorities and himself subject to possible future prosecution.

The man told me to sod off, thus confirming his excellent command of the English language. He then summoned a passing policeman, who, once appraised of the situation, marched me off to his car where I spent the next twenty minutes being lectured along the lines that in the unlikely event of Qatar wanting to enforce its parking regulations, then their preference was to do it themselves.

My reason for relating this incident is to illustrate that Qatar is no different from anywhere else. It's not what you know, it's who you know. I have another example.

Shortly after leaving the police car, I was involved in a minor road accident when a van hit me from behind at one of the roundabouts on the Doha ring road. To date, wishing to avoid undue concern to my family and friends, I've dodged any detailed reference to what occurs on the roads in this country. But no longer. Now seems as good a time as any to reveal the truth. I'll get back to the accident shortly.

Should you believe in living life in the fast lane, then Qatar's the place for you. Driving on the roads here can be a hazardous business, with some modifications in style essential if you're to live to see your next oil change. But what are these essential modifications?

In Britain, the side of the road you drive a vehicle is largely dictated by the Highway Code – and what everyone else is doing. In Qatar, no such unimportant restrictions apply. Just because most people are driving along in one direction, is no reason to refrain from sailing merrily along in the other. Likewise, the speed limit here is determined not by the law, but by the maximum speed your vehicle can achieve. If your car will go at 100 miles an hour, then that's the speed limit.

Employing only one hand is another essential adjustment necessary for successful driving. The other should either be dangled out through the window – ideally the one next to you – or kept in constant proximity to the horn to ensure the surrounding noise level remains at a minimum of 150 decibels. And using indicators must be assiduously avoided. Such recklessness would not only establish an unwelcome precedent, but jeopardise that ingredient of unpredictability which is such an intrinsic feature of life – or, if you're not careful, death – in Qatar.

And now parking. This is another skill which demands meticulous attention, it being crucial that your vehicle is parked at such an angle, or in such a position, as to instantly produce a traffic tailback of at least 2 miles. Anything less is considered inept.

Most visitors here can recall a specific incident which first alerted them to the wisdom of adopting a more flexible and aggressive attitude towards driving than they would normally apply at home. And I well remember mine. Travelling along the Doha to Umm Said highway at what I considered a fair old pace, I was overtaken by the Bangladeshi school bus loaded with around fifty singing children most of whom cheered in obvious derision at what they perceived as my stately progress. Damn cheek!

But the scene most indicative of driving in Qatar, can be witnessed daily at any of the few sets of traffic lights to be found in Doha.

Unlike Britain, where a driver is rarely required to wait unduly before traffic lights change from red to green, here they are set so delays approaching four minutes are common and lengthy queues of vehicles often form. When observing a line of traffic moving away at lights in Britain, you see the gradual delay factor. The further a vehicle is from the front the more it is delayed and sometimes the lights will have actually reverted to red before any forward progress is made. In Qatar, things are different. Immediately the green light appears, every vehicle in the queue – perhaps half a mile long – will move forward simultaneously amid a cacophony of hooting and arm waving, and woe betide anyone who hesitates. It's like the grid at Silverstone for the start of the British Grand Prix.

Some weeks ago, mine was the front car in the queue at the Doha Airport lights and the wait was so interminable I fell asleep. A big mistake. You cannot imagine the tirade of sound which awoke me the instant the lights changed to green. Or maybe you can. I'd need a volume of Biblical proportions to record every piece of advice proffered to me at that moment in at least seven languages, not all of them recognised by the United Nations. And to compound my misfortune, the vehicle behind mine proved to be that of the Qatari police who promptly arrested me and insisted on my immediate transportation to the police station in their car, leaving mine where it stood by the lights. The upshot of this was an instantaneous and ear-splitting accumulation of vehicles from all accessible directions.

Luckily the police were extremely understanding. I was taken to see the captain, whose brother not only lived about two miles from my own London home, but also had the misfortune to support Arsenal – my own club, which has bored me to death for the past twenty years. Extravagant production of my Supporters' Club card hastily resolved the whole thing in handshakes and smiles, and a warning not to nod off again in such imprudent circumstances. Up the Gunners.

I was free to go, but not before being sentenced to a joke from the captain. Presumably it came from his brother in London, and as an example of the appalling punishments which can be inflicted upon the transgressor in Qatar, I shall relate the thing. It's not my usual practice to do jokes, but this was official state business.

Two Arabs were travelling on camels through the desert, eight days from the nearest civilisation.

Abdul to Khalid. 'Spurs lost again then.'

Khalid to Abdul. 'How do you know?'

Abdul to Khalid. 'It's Saturday afternoon.'

Not too bad was it? Anyway, it beats ten days in jail.

Laughing heartily, in my case with commendable conviction, the police drove me as close as they could get to my car. Which was a mile, as for some inexplicable reason a quite gigantic traffic jam had formed.

Now where was I? I'd just been belted from behind this evening at one of the roundabouts on the Doha ring road. This is a regular venue for mishaps as the highways here are all three lanes wide, whilst the connecting roundabouts have only two lanes – a system which even in Britain would cause problems, but in Qatar makes life insurance the business to be in.

The law here, which is strictly enforced, requires any vehicle involved in an accident, however minor, to remain immobile at the scene until the police arrive. There being no such thing as a minor accident in Qatar, and with the majority occurring at roundabouts, colossal traffic jams ensue, the inevitable consequence of which is to prevent the police from quickly reaching the unfortunate victims. This further contributes to the disruption.

On this occasion, it took fifty minutes for the officer to arrive and in accordance with standard procedure the van driver and I surrendered our driving licences and accompanied him to the police station where, using a method somewhat more arbitrary and instantaneous than would apply in Britain, he becomes judge and jury to establish responsibility for the accident. This is crucial for purposes of vehicle insurance as whoever gets the fateful thumbs down must take responsibility for all repair costs.

Not that being the innocent party necessarily resolves the

matter, as Vincent found last week. I met him by chance at the post-office where he mentioned his involvement in a minor road accident for which he was declared blameless.

'So what happened to the prayers?' I enquired quite reasonably.

'More bad if no pray,' came the admirable reply.

His understanding of English has improved perceptibly during recent weeks. Seemingly, he's taking lessons from his young son. Good for him. And he's still got his cold although, evidently, not the same one. Maybe he should add virus protection to his prayer list. On checking his insurance policy, which doubtless was with one of the less reputable companies, Vincent discovered the small print revealed conditions waiving all liability unless the accident occurred in a snowstorm on a Tuesday morning, and with a ninety-three year old, one-legged man driving a red and white striped Porsche. Or something very similar.

However, in this instance, as I'd been hit from behind whilst stationary at a roundabout, I was quietly confident of being absolved of all responsibility – the fact the other driver was an Arab having no effect on the correct dispensation of justice and the law. An open and shut case if ever I saw one. Who am I kidding?

For several minutes, the policeman and van driver discussed the incident in confidential tones, looking towards me at regular intervals as if I was a cockroach. And with increasing suspicion. Despite my lack of Arabic, I could detect my innocence wasn't an opinion they necessarily shared, and my version of events wasn't likely to be required to assist the proceedings either. I had a fair idea where things were heading.

The officer turned towards me. The verdict, democratically and unanimously reached, was the whole thing was my fault. This was evidently based on the sound principle that if I hadn't been in Qatar in the first place, the accident would never have occurred. As I said before it's not what you know, it's who you know.

IF THE SUN DOESN'T KILL YOU,

I protested, of course, and waved my Arsenal Supporters Club card at them. Desperate times – desperate measures. (That's a well-worn cliché.) After several minutes of dark mutterings, critical headshaking and wild gesticulations – mine, of course – it was acknowledged the matter would officially be declared an act of God. This meant I cough up my costs while the other dimwit pays for his, which was fine by me as he sustained most of the damage. But it's strange. That card has already done more for me here than it ever did in London.

Having arranged for a hired replacement, I drove to my local garage and deposited the car for the necessary minor repairs. When the hired vehicle arrived, I instantly spotted the radio aerial had been snapped off and only the bottom few inches remained. As an effective and loud car radio is essential in Qatar to complement the helpful advice frequently offered by fellow drivers, I drew this defect to the attention of the hire company's representative as he attempted to depart in some haste.

'No problem.'

'No problem? But this aerial is useless. Why no problem?'

'Because the car's got no radio.'

There are some days, and this has certainly been one of them, when it just doesn't pay to get up. Joan of Arc said that.

* * * * *

Qatar is a place, wherever one goes, one expects to see goats. It's not that they reside here in prodigious numbers, but they do seem to move about a lot.

I said that to Robin Day on the telephone last week when asked how I'd characterise life here. A nice girl, Robin. I went to school with her in North London. She's married now to an ex-missionary from Zimbabwe and they live over a chip shop in Huddersfield with fourteen cats and a stuffed wildebeest. Or was it fourteen wildebeests and a stuffed cat? No matter.

My point is it's often easy to portray Qatar as being just a little closer to the Dark Ages than is confirmed by reality. There are numerous examples of impressive late-twentieth century technology, which when combined with illustrations of contrasting nature, blend to retain the perpetual element of surprise which is such an endearing aspect of the Qatari lifestyle.

The public telephone system, for example, is an extremely modern one with all national calls permitted free of charge, and its efficiency could demonstrate a few things to some of its European equivalents. Even here, however, complications with the telephone aren't unknown and this evening I've twice become involved in curious conversations which perfectly exemplify the vicissitudes of life in Qatar.

The first occurred around seven o'clock as I was halfway through cleaning most of a cheese omelette off the kitchen floor.

'Is that 885680?' said an English, female voice. Before allowing me time to say that it wasn't, the voice continued,

'Are you aware of our group, the Expat Senior Citizens of Qatar?'

Rather taken aback at the question I replied, 'No madam, not by name I'm afraid, but I'd probably recognise a few if I saw them shuffling along the street.'

'No, no, no,' the woman said, somewhat impatiently I thought, 'I'm afraid we're in a bit of a spot.'

'Well, I'm sorry to hear that,' I commiserated, 'but I'm not sure what I can do – not at this late stage.'

'No you don't understand,' the woman continued, by now becoming quite unnecessarily agitated. 'The local Health Minister was due to talk to us concerning the prevention of AIDS, but has gone sick and we'd like you to speak to the Expat Senior Citizens of Qatar on Tuesday.'

'Well,' I said, trying to sound worthy of the honour, 'I'll

speak to anyone if they'll speak to me. But what can I tell them they didn't lose interest in years ago?'

I was about to raise the subject of a fee, after all philanthropy doesn't come cheap these days, when she asked in a most distressed tone of voice,

'I suppose that is the British Embassy, isn't it?'

'Good gracious no,' I replied. 'I'm Peter Wood, the well-known international business man.'

'That's as may be,' the woman snapped, 'but not well-known enough.'

The silence that followed indicated the abrupt end to my association with the Expat Senior Citizens of Qatar. I hope it was nothing I said.

The second call this evening came at around eleven o'clock when a rude, continental-sounding man phoned, whom I naturally assumed to be French. He demanded a smart, clean taxi to collect him from home at five o'clock tomorrow morning. Carefully noting the man's address and phone number, I promised to be punctual and take extreme care not to disturb his chickens.

An hour later, at midnight, I called the number back, and was halfway through explaining my washing machine was spewing water across the kitchen floor and required immediate attention, when the same man interrupted me and bawled, 'This isn't a bloody plumber's, you idiot.'

'Really?' I replied. 'And this isn't a bloody taxi firm.'

The first call I made up. The second one I didn't.

It's 25 December. Six o'clock in the morning. No holiday here, of course, where Christmas is unrecognised. For the next eighteen hours I'll be at the seaport where a ship is due to discharge heavy construction equipment. But I've just enjoyed one of life's simple but fulfilling experiences.

Shortly before dawn, which was an hour ago, I walked about half a mile into the desert to watch the sunrise. Following behind were both the Scarfaces and, to my surprise, three of the goats, the whole lot strung out in a line behind me with only Arsenal apparently not fancying the stroll. I felt like the Pied Piper. Even a couple of the chickens made a commendable effort before their physical limitations forced them to quit.

For nearly an hour we all sat around in tranquil isolation, listening to the Sibelius 2nd Symphony drifting from a tiny cassette player Moira has lent me. Whether as a consequence of the early hour, or the music, the animals behaved impeccably – even the goats refraining from any inappropriate activity. As the sun rose inexorably above the horizon, even Doha seemed a world away, let alone London.

'We must do this again next year,' I told the gang as we all trooped back to the villa.

Five minutes ago, whilst striding into the courtyard to feed the chickens and reveal to them the fate which befalls so many of their sisters around the world on this special day – just so they understand who's in charge here – I all but trod on a Christmas present lying by the doorstep. It was from one of the goats and was still steaming.

8

Dear Kylie, I think of you in the desert with completely nothing on.

Warning. This chapter contains material which may be considered offensive to the French.

There have been a number of significant dates in the annals of Qatar. On 18 January 1940, the first oil was discovered; on 3 September 1971, independence from Britain was declared; and on 3 September 1991, the largest natural gas field in the world commenced production.

But the eminence of these illustrious events has now been superseded by the announcement in yesterday's *Gulf Times* of the inauguration that evening, 8 January 1992, of Qatar's first take-away pizza restaurant.

'Grand opening tonight,' screamed the advertisement, 'with an amazing selection of numerous pizzas to suit everyone. To take away or sit in on, our restaurant is the last word in luxury and comfort.' Disregarding the point that the last word in luxury and comfort is, in fact, comfort, I read on. 'Visit us for unrivalled choices. Situated next to the Ministry of Information and Culture office. Open 7:00 pm.'

It was soon after seven o'clock when I arrived outside the Ministry to join about 5,000 others all looking confused and enquiring of each other if they had the remotest inkling as to the location of this new pizza restaurant. The whereabouts of the Ministry was clearly evident as there it stood in its white stone magnificence, a tribute to superglue if ever I saw one. But where was this much vaunted takeaway with its infinite supply of pizzas?

It was the night porter at the Ministry who eventually revealed the existence of a second Information and Culture Office on the other side of town, the location of which he helpfully indicated by pointing in the direction of the rest of Qatar. By now, the initial enthusiasm of the multitude had long since diminished and most headed home for a tinned mutton curry. So the feeding of the 5,000 it wasn't. Nevertheless, prompted by my British resolve, the remnants of we more determined pizza hunters, including one daft fanatic with a fork lift truck, resumed our vehicular search across Doha. You four men go that way. The rest follow me.

It was almost nine o'clock when we located the restaurant. Frankly, it was difficult to miss. Precisely what was in the mind of the architect, I can't imagine. Assuming he had one in the first place.

Single-storey and constructed in orange and grey brick, its flat roof supported a wooden tower three times the height of the building. At its crown, an immense cheese and tomato pizza had been attached. Sadly, in the brisk wind this appendage was proving less secure than its owners must have wished, with the pizza flapping enthusiastically and looking ready to take off in the general direction of Kuwait. To offset this, an intrepid member of staff was clinging grimly at the top, violently swinging a mallet in an ill-considered attempt to persuade it to stay. As a consequence of this frenzied activity, the tower itself had begun tilting at a perceptibly doubtful angle. It's the leaning tower of pizza, I thought.

Inside, things looked distinctly more controlled. A cluster of immaculately clad waiters stood by, their shirts all whiter than mine and their trouser-creases visibly sharper. And were the extravagant claims made in yesterday's *Gulf Times* justified? Indeed they were. But there is, however, a limit to everything.

I was presented with a menu of gargantuan proportions and by the time I'd reached the thirty-fifth page of unrivalled choices, had begun losing interest in the whole affair. Surrendering, I took the easy option. Cheese and tomato.

Grabbing the menu, the waiter scanned the pages.

'One number 144,' he shouted to the chef in the kitchen.

'What's a 144?' came the reply.

'Cheese and tomato,' bawled back the waiter, who then looked at me and enquired, 'small, medium or large?'

To his evident surprise I requested the large.

'Are you with a coach party, sir? If not, I think maybe the small size will be sufficient.'

'No, I'm feeling particularly hungry. Definitely the large, please.'

'One large,' the waiter yelled to the kitchen.

'One large what?' roared back the chef.

'One large 144?'

'What's a 144?'

'Cheese and tomato.'

Ten minutes later, two men staggered from the kitchen with the pizza.

'Is it to take away, sir?' one of them asked, casting an apprehensive glance at the dimensions of the restaurant door.

It was ten o'clock when I finally lurched into the villa with the pizza. It would have been even later had I not received some unexpected assistance. And they say you can never find a fork lift truck when you need one.

* * * * *

Just twelve hours ago I stared death in the face. But I survived. Thanks to my bathroom door.

THE WASHING MACHINE WILL

It was two o'clock this morning the drama began. Probably in reaction to stuffing myself full of hard-won pizza just a few hours earlier. I had trouble sleeping and was regretting the greed, that childhood caution – your eyes are bigger than your belly – returning to haunt me.

It was then my attention was drawn to a rustling sound from the lounge, soon followed by a second and then by a third. Knowing the room to be empty but being of a fearless disposition, I decided to investigate and so entered the lounge, switched on the light and listened – to silence. Then suddenly, out of the corner of my eye, I saw one of the cats dart from under the curtains and hide behind the sofa. Ah, a simple explanation, I thought.

However, I was about to pull the sofa from the wall to remove the cat before returning to bed, when a quite dreadful realisation hit me. That wasn't a cat. It was the size of a cat, and it had fur like a cat. But its tail wasn't right – it was a long, thin, furless tail, a bit like a . . . My God, it's a bloody rat!!!

For a moment I stood transfixed, then scarpered to the bedroom for my steel-capped boots.

OK, I thought. Now look at this logically. At the moment this thing seems reluctant to meet me in a face-to-face confrontation. And very accommodating of it. With my boots luring me into an ill-considered measure of self-confidence, I plodded decisively back to the lounge.

My first move was to quickly close all internal doors in the villa, with the exception of the lounge door which opens straight on to the outside courtyard. This offered the rat a single avenue of escape. Lassoing the arm of the sofa with some string to maximise the distance between myself and the rat, I jerked the sofa from the wall confident the intruder would immediately run in the only logical direction – outside. Unfortunately, the rat had obviously failed its Masters Degree in Logic and shot out from the sofa at the speed of light, running in the exact opposite direction to that intended. It crashed with the impact of a missile into the bedroom door, the corner of which split like a burst tyre allowing the rat to enter. OK, I thought. It's one up to the rat. What now?

Isolation was the immediate priority. I ensured the brute couldn't escape from the bedroom by putting a large bucket against the hole in the door which I weighted with a packet of onions. I next carefully considered the two obvious options left to me – either leave immediately for London, or phone the landlord. I plumped for the latter. But it was a close decision.

Initially, the response was far from encouraging. In fact there wasn't one. But after ringing for around three minutes, the telephone was finally answered.

'zzzzzzzzzz.'

'Is that Mr Al-Khalifi?'

'Gone away,' mumbled a drowsy voice.

This was puzzling as only a few hours earlier we'd discussed a problem concerning the goats and that tiny cassette player Moira had lent me. They've eaten it. Undeterred I pressed on.

'This is Mr Peter at the villa. Can I speak to Mr Al-Khalifi please? It's urgent.'

'Yes, yes, it's me,' he grunted, with a marked lack of interest, the word urgent having as much impact as you'd expect around here. Outlining the situation, I awaited his response.

'Have you any idea of the time? It's only a rat. What size is it?'

'Well you know what a camel looks like? Forget the humps and that's it.'

'Oh, all right. Give me ten minutes and I'll arrange something.'

Twenty minutes later three men arrived in a truck, two brandishing sticks and the third clutching a blow torch. Good grief, I thought, they're going to grill the thing to death. After receiving as detailed a briefing of the situation as their lack of English allowed, matters got underway.

Now all armed with sticks, the three men formed a huddle to discuss tactics and after a short pause for prayers and three cups of tea, they began their advance with sticks outraised, reminiscent of the Three Musketeers. From my vantage point on the table, I had a perfect view as their leader flung open the bedroom door and they charged fearlessly inside.

A split second later out shot the rat like the target at a clay pigeon shoot. With all exit routes closed, it impacted at about 130 miles an hour into the middle of the bathroom door which shuddered, but held firm. The rat fell on the spot, and from my new position high on top of the freezer, I saw it roll over on its back – either dead, or comatose.

It was a further ten seconds before the musketeers emerged, their failure to locate the prey in the bedroom clearly a mystery to them. Calling down, I indicated the rat was lying prone at the far end of the hallway and they immediately dashed to the spot with rekindled enthusiasm, clearly intent on beating the living daylights out of it.

Despite thrashing around for the next five minutes at their immobile target, none of the men in their frenzied euphoria managed to inflict any further damage. I told them to remove the creature and like a trio of conquering gladiators, they carried it out in triumph, borne precariously on a 1988 edition of the Qatari telephone directory.

The men left at three o'clock. Whilst locking up, I thought I detected a slight movement in the prostrate shape of the rat in the courtyard.

At daybreak it was gone. So perhaps it was only stunned after all, or maybe it was eaten by the cats, or more than likely they've both been eaten by the rat. So if it is still alive, I guess it's every animal for itself out there now. Come to think of it, I haven't seen any of the goats since yesterday.

✻ ✻ ✻ ✻ ✻

IF THE SUN DOESN'T KILL YOU,

Today is Valentine's Day and my MD in London has kindly sent a card. Not for me, you understand, but to me, at my request. I fancied despatching a spoof card to Kylie and there would be as much chance of locating a Valentine's card in Qatar as one celebrating the Jewish New Year.

During recent weeks I've become friendly with Kylie's husband Kurt, who's visited the villa on a couple of occasions as we have a similar predilection for rock music and blast away together into the night. He has the adjoining mail-box to mine at the central post-office in Doha and we often collide in the mornings when collecting our post. No such thing as mail deliveries in Qatar, of course.

It came as some surprise to both of us to discover we each knew Kylie. Kurt is endlessly bemoaning her endearing but irksome little ways. The latter I can believe.

'But you must make allowances,' he explained, 'she comes from a broken home. Mind you, it was probably her that broke it.'

Last week he was lamenting her extraordinary talent for tidying things away in such a fashion as to subsequently render them impossible to find. Something which takes Kylie a minute to clear away, takes Kurt thirty to locate and anything taking two minutes, is lost forever. Kurt reckons she could park the car in the garage so adroitly he could search all day and still not come across it.

I saw them both in the Souq last Friday. Imagine, I thought, an Australian called Kylie and a German named Kurt. Aren't there any surprises left in the world?

It was intriguing to discover they were both thirty years old and share the same birthday. Or I found it intriguing. Just imagine the odds against meeting an Australian who was born on the same day in the same year as yourself and wants to marry you. I'm banking on the odds against it happening to me being at least nil. And to compound the coincidences, Moira is also thirty and only two days older than Kylie and Kurt. The Lord moves in mysterious ways.

THE WASHING MACHINE WILL

Wearing a long, black dress and carrying a spade, Kylie looked even more forbidding in the Souq than when I'd seen her previously at Moira's for the rugby final. She and Kurt are a discordant couple, somewhat evocative of Blackpool postcard characters. Kylie is tall, approaching six feet, and strikingly thin. I've always considered myself scrawny, but she takes things to excess.

Kurt is different altogether. Of barely average height and weighing around fifteen stones, his most athletic days are doubtless behind him – as is much of the fifteen stones. Having myself worked many years for a Hamburg company and made frequent visits to Germany where I've several good friends, I'm certainly no believer in the stereotype male German. In my experience, aside from all wearing leather shorts, playing accordions, and sporting little black moustaches, they're no different from any other nation. No. That was unforgiveably cheap. I apologise. However, with Kurt, there's some minor justification for this view as he certainly wears leather shorts at home and also owns a concertina on which he can play 'Born To Run'. That impressed me. Whether Springsteen would have been equally enthused is maybe open to doubt. Which brings me nicely back to the Valentine's Day card.

Inside I wrote:

> When I'm feeling sad and blue
> And I know I can't go on,
> I think of you in the desert
> With completely nothing on.

With Kurt's prior knowledge, I shoved it inside their post-box this morning. Later he phoned to report Kylie was delighted to have received the card – which frankly doesn't say much for either of us.

See you in playschool.

* * * * *

I didn't tell you earlier as I've been keeping it as a surprise, but today has been the twentieth anniversary of the accession of the Emir of Qatar. It has been a holiday and this afternoon I briefly watched a procession through Doha of around twenty-five floats which honoured the occasion. Mainly cultural in tone, they were nevertheless of a commendable standard and much effort had obviously been expended in their preparation. This evening a celebratory fireworks display was held along the seafront which resulted in a most curious episode on Qatar Radio which I'll come to later.

I didn't attend the display. Never enamoured by bangers and Catherine-wheels even as a boy, and having watched the definitive Jean Michel Jarre laser and fireworks concert in London a couple of years back, the counter-attraction of completing a mound of ironing proved too great. But Vincent telephoned and considered it rattlingly good. Mind you, he's easily pleased. Oh, and his cold is no better. But thanks for asking.

Although not watching the fireworks, from inside the villa I could clearly hear them exploding. So could the livestock and, disturbed by the din, they became understandably restless. The chickens were participating in some form of synchronised flapping giving a passable impression of a prototype Mexican wave. Meanwhile Scarface 2, always excessively emotional, became involved in a nasty altercation with Arsenal, the instigator of most of the trouble around here. What seems to have occurred, or as best I could establish from the post-fight interviews, was that having crept up behind the goat, probably on some kind of revenge mission, the cat clobbered it over the head with an adjustable spanner. More or less.

Inside, the ironing was into its second hour as I listened to Tim Manns on the radio.

'And now, "Everything I Do I Do It For You", by Bryan Adams. Still in the charts after fourteen consecutive years at number one. And listen out at the end of the record when I'll be setting a competition with two free tickets for a performance at the local theatre tomorrow night, by the Romanian Youth String Orchestra.'

Together with the rest of Qatar, I waited breathlessly for the record to end, none of us wishing to forgo such an enticing opportunity.

Then at last . . . 'and everything I do I do it for you'. The record concluded. And this is the point at which the afore-mentioned curious episode shows up. Because nothing happened. Just silence. Other than the sound of the stylus as it clicked itself repeatedly around the final groove from which there was no escape.

Two minutes, five minutes, ten minutes. I gave it a full twenty before calling the studio on the telephone. But no reply. What's going on, Tim?

Restraining my disappointment at apparently losing the chance of seeing the Romanian Youth String Orchestra, the only consolation being it looked likely no one else was going either, I completed the ironing, accompanied by Chas and Dave on the cassette player. But what were the circum-stances in the studio? With the record still rotating on the turntable, there was certainly no power failure.

During the ensuing thirty minutes, I twice more checked back to the radio but click, click, click, was the only sound. Let's hope the stylus shop opens promptly in the morning.

By now it was time for the closedown of normal trans-mission so no immediate resolution of the mystery was likely. But what had happened? Where was Tim? And where was the producer of the show, and at least two technicians who I know attend the studio during the broadcast? A minimum of four people had disappeared without trace. This was the *Marie Celeste* of radio.

It was two hours after the aborted programme I finally contacted Tim and he disclosed the entirely logical circumstances which fashioned this evening's events. Logical, that is, as seen from Qatar.

Aside from himself, in the studio with Tim for the show this evening had been a producer and two Indian technicians. When the fireworks display began, which could clearly be heard inside the studio, one of the technicians opted to slip outside for a few moments to watch. When he hadn't reappeared ten minutes later, Tim sent the second technician outside to find him. But after a further five minutes he also had failed to return. By now Tim was becoming irritated, waiting, as he was, to set the Romanian Orchestra competition and the two technicians were required to answer phone-calls from the eager, thronging masses. So he sent the producer outside to order them both to return immediately. And you can guess what happened next. Nothing. He didn't reappear either.

At this juncture Tim was alone in the studio and, indeed, the building. Choosing the Bryan Adams track which is nearly seven minutes long and would allow sufficient time away from the microphone, he dived outside to establish the whereabouts of the three men.

Once in the street, he saw them about thirty yards away clustered together in conversation. Flinging his arms in the direction of the studio door and shouting an appropriate invitation to return, Tim hurried to re-enter the building before the record had finished.

At the door was a policeman.

'See pass, pleese.'

'Pass? I don't have pass. I work here.'

'Must see pass, pleese.'

'I've not been given pass. Please let me in I'm doing broadcast.'

'Must see pass before go in, pleese. Or no go in.'

So there it is. Once each of the four men had left the building, re-entry had been refused without production of a pass with which none of them had been issued. It transpired additional security was in operation due to the accession day celebrations, resulting in this touch of over-zealousness from an officer who was only doing his job, mate. But the most perturbing aspect of the entire evening was I had no opportunity to get tickets to see the Romanian Youth String Orchestra.

Tim told me his brother was born on 5 November and was nine years old before realising the fireworks every year weren't just for his benefit. I'm not altogether sure I believe that.

Before me is today's *Gulf Times* which includes two articles pertaining to the accession day celebrations of yesterday.

The first concerns my lamentation at missing the performance by the youthful Romanians. Sadly, so will everyone else because they're not coming. Transportation problems, according to *The Gulf Times*. Probably the wrong sort of snow on the line outside Bucharest.

The second article is an understated account of yesterday's procession of floats. It's curious how you don't fully appreciate things at the time. I now regret not staying longer.

The 20th Accession Anniversary of His Highness The Emir Sheikh Khalifa Bin Hamad Al-Thani climaxed with a wonderful and colourful pageant along the Doha Corniche. Large, exuberant and cheering crowds watched with enthusiasm and excitement as the flotilla of imaginative and colourfully decorated vehicles wound their way majestically along the imposing waterfront.

Decorative floats bedecked with magnificently coloured flowers and belonging to and representing various Ministries and private companies depicted the country's outstanding achievements, development and progress.

The impressive procession was flogged [*I think you mean flagged, Mr Editor*] off at the Doha club and ended in triumph with more excited crowds at the Exhibition Centre.

It was a pageant which everyone who saw it will remember.

I'm saying nothing.

* * * * *

All things considered, the condition of the roads in Qatar appears of a quite acceptable standard providing, that is, you view them at a height of at least three miles from the safety of a 747. Any closer inspection is likely to reveal an assortment of holes of sufficient depth to conceal Sunderland. And yesterday one of them brought Vincent's latest sideline as a motorcyclist to an unexpected conclusion.

Knowing me to have owned a 500 c.c. Triumph back in the seventies, and under the misguided impression this indicated some knowledge of the subject on my part, Vincent phoned me last month and, amidst a salvo of sneezing, solicited my assistance in respect of a second-hand bike he proposed to buy from the one and only motorcycle shop in Qatar. Perhaps describing this place as a motorcycle shop is an exaggeration as it's actually the local hairdressing salon which has diversified.

Having arrived at the premises, Vincent and I were directed by the owner to a tiny scrapyard at the rear crammed high with parts of rusty old bikes, parts for rusty old bikes, and parts for parts of rusty old bikes. But only one complete bike. And that was rusty. Lacking a front headlamp, the mudguards and a visible braking system, both its tyres were flat.

The owner soon joined us, having bumped into practically every piece of wreckage in the yard. Appearing so short-sighted as to raise serious questions concerning the safety and general well-being of his salon clientele, he peered at us quizzically and then at the bike.

'Very good value for the price, sirs.'

'Does it go?'

'No, not really.'

'What's wrong with it?'

'More or less everything.'

As the asking price was approximately nothing, Vincent had little to lose but his life and so became the proud owner of this mobile offence. Even in Qatar it was probably against the law to be within 100 yards of the thing. At least on a Monday.

The following four weeks brought the bike's various deficiencies into conspicuous evidence. Pre-eminent amongst these was its irritating practice of unloading its battery in the road without warning whilst Vincent was belting around Doha. The upshot of this was a series of alarming explosions which on three occasions to my certain knowledge resulted in the mobilisation of half the Qatari Air Force. This persistent commotion became so severe that after two visits to the villa I had no alternative but to insist he parked the bike some 500 yards away, as most of the live-stock were becoming disorientated. Scarface 2 trembled for days after his last call. Actually I'm becoming a little con-cerned about the poor cat as he's recently developed a nasty cough. I hope he hasn't started smoking.

It was precisely a month after its acquisition that Vincent yesterday rode his motorcycle into a ridiculous hole in the Doha ring road from which it never re-emerged as a com-plete entity. He was mortified but unhurt. It's true to say there aren't many motorcyclists to be seen around Qatar where they enjoy the status and lifespan of a blind hedgehog on the M4. So maybe it was for the best.

But long gone are the days when a citizen of the United Kingdom like myself could afford to be condescending concerning the condition of another country's roads, with so many of Britain's highways – as I recall when last bouncing around London – resembling a motorcross course. Today, British holes can match those of almost any country in the world, although for sheer depth and longevity maybe not Qatar.

Which brings me to my Aunt Gwendoline. And what possible connection does she have with holes in Qatar? Quite frankly, not a lot. But Vincent's misfortune brings to mind that some years ago my Aunt, who's barmy in the extreme, negotiated her Morris Minor into a hole in Milford Haven High Street from which she found it impossible to withdraw. To do so would have involved engaging reverse gear, a move not once attempted during her thirty-eight years of sedate pottering through south-west Wales. So she left the car where it stood and took the bus home.

With all and sundry in Milford Haven fully aware Aunt Gwendoline was as nutty as a fruitcake, the spectacle of the forsaken car was considered a matter of scant concern. It was only two days later when my Uncle enquired of her as to the whereabouts of the vehicle, that the incident came to light and he was able to extricate it from its semi-subterranean predicament.

The last news I heard of my Aunt, she was under questioning by her local police. And not for the first time. Some years ago she was suspected of involvement in a series of arson attacks on accordion players in the area, which, while both reprehensible and in breach of Common Market regulations, indicated a prejudice I can more readily appreciate since the Albanian fiasco. At least I think it was accordion players. However, on this occasion, she'd tipped off the station sergeant that my Uncle was a member of the 'Keep Wales For the Welsh Society' and had placed an incendiary device in the local Woolworths. They'd cleared the store and my Uncle was being interviewed by the Bomb Squad, before doubts surfaced as to the reliability of the information after Aunt Gwendoline re-contacted the police station to inform them their Chief Constable was the 'Mr Big' behind the Society. But I may have digressed a little from the point.

A visiting business colleague this morning asked my opinion concerning the best way to drive in Qatar. Quite honestly, very carefully is the best way to drive. Otherwise you're liable to disappear without trace down one of these holes. A significant number of road accidents result from drivers attempting emergency action to avoid this inconvenience and consequently colliding with others who, in all probability, were undertaking a precisely similar manoeuvre.

If such a misfortune occurs, perhaps causing a trifling dent in the vehicle's bodywork, or a broken rear light lens, then Qatari officialdom is primed to leap into action.

Any damage sustained by a vehicle involved in an accident, however minor, must be registered with the police and an appropriate form is then supplied to record the circumstances and the resulting defect. This form, issued by the policeman in charge of dents, smashed lenses and other miscellaneous imperfections, must be retained by the owner of the dent etcetera, until such time as repairs are effected. And if you sustain such damage and a nice policeman stops you on the road and says,

'Hello, chummy, can I see your authorisation to be in possession of that dent?' then you'd better produce the form. Otherwise expect a late dinner. Which makes one wonder if driving in Qatar warrants all the subsequent bother. There is, however, one conspicuous advantage.

There are various methods of travelling in these parts, and cars don't monopolise the roads as they do in Britain. Hence more space, no parking problems, and no traffic wardens. Which is just as well. It's not easy sticking a parking ticket on a camel.

I thank you.

* * * * *

IF THE SUN DOESN'T KILL YOU,

So what would you do in Britain if you lost all electrical power in your home at six o'clock on a Sunday morning? I'll tell you one thing you wouldn't do and that's persuade your local electricity company to come out to repair it. No chance. Should you prove fortunate enough to find their non-business hours telephone number, you might get a recorded message telling you to bugger off till Monday. But on a Saturday or Sunday, forget it.

But given this situation, I'll tell you what happens in Qatar – a country with no piped gas, making electricity the sole power source in most homes.

At around six o'clock one Friday morning last month, I lost all electrical power in the villa, a rare but serious inconvenience in an environment where air conditioning and refrigeration are essential.

When this occurred, initially indicated by my fax machine fainting in mid-transmission, my immediate reaction was to suspect the goats whose eating habits continue to be an embarrassing inconvenience. But a rapid search outside found them all innocently asleep on the roof. How in heaven's name do they get up there? Responsibility therefore clearly lay in a more inanimate and less malodorous direction.

If I may veer momentarily from the point, the acquisition of this fax machine led to a most unusual dialogue with the shop assistant which demonstrates that even the most implausible of assertions can subsequently prove accurate.

Having returned to the villa with my newly purchased machine, I began the installation procedure using the manual provided. Before long, it became apparent that some of the machine's features didn't correspond precisely with those shown in the instructions. Similar, but not exact. Clearly the manual, which had not been packed inside the box but supplied separately by the assistant, wasn't the appropriate one for the machine.

Returning to the shop, I spoke with the same man and

following the accustomed pleasantries involving seats and tea, advised him,

'You've given me the wrong manual. This refers to another model. Please change the manual for the correct one.'

'No problem. Hold on. I check.'

Returning two minutes later,

'No. You definitely got right manual. It's wrong machine you got. I change machine.'

Wrong machine? Piffle. This man's an idiot.

'Don't be silly. How can I have the wrong machine? I came into your shop and chose the fax machine I wanted – the only one in stock. I then took it home. So explain to me how I can possibly have the wrong machine but the right manual.'

And do you know he did? I'd been given a model set for European power supply systems which is slightly adapted when sold the Middle East. But the manual was the relevant version for this part of the world. So the assistant was correct. The words egg and face came immediately to mind. Back quickly to my power loss in the villa.

The next move was to check my electrical power box on which was printed a telephone number to ring 'in case of troublesome problem'. I called the number. After two rings a man answered and requested my power box identification reference, essential for locating the villa's position in a country which lacks detailed street maps. Eight minutes later four men arrived, offered me a Coke and chapatti and quickly located the fault in an outside junction box. And within twenty minutes of my original call, full power was restored. Not a bad service. And can you imagine that happening in Britain at six o'clock on a Sunday morning? Answers on a postcard please, to 'Camels May Fly Competition', Doha, Qatar.

And that's not all. Two weeks later, on receiving my electricity bill, I noted a small reduction as compensation for my 'Disconnection of Supply'. All of thirty minutes. So one up to Qatar. Not to imply criticism of the British electricity companies who could reasonably argue their substantially higher labour costs would prohibit the viability of such a service, albeit some frustrated customers may see this as an incongruous justification in view of the handsome profits made by these companies.

But wait. I must not be controversial. My horoscope in this morning's *Gulf Times* advised me to avoid becoming involved in arguments. So today I'm being especially uncontroversial.

Actually this horoscope also urged me to go and work in a cool climate where I would apparently meet a fine, honourable woman who would distract me from the fourth onwards. The fourth what I wonder?

However, in the Woman's section of the same edition of *The Gulf Times* there was another horoscope which suggested I should have a fling and buy myself a new dress. It also warned I'm liable to have trouble with the man in my life.

So, taking everything into consideration, I think I'll forget all about horoscopes from now on.

By the way. Also in this morning's *Gulf Times* it stated the temperature yesterday in Qatar was 118° centigrade with sun and occasional heat haze. I wonder how we survived?

The Gulf Times. Order your copy today.

Incidentally, I omitted the material about the French. I've just heard on BBC World Service we stuffed them in yesterday's rugby international in Paris. And that will do me.

9

You wait twelve days for a sink and then two come along together.

It's the first day of the Holy month of Ramadan which commemorates the period when the Koran was first revealed to the Prophet Mohammad. During this month all Muslims, other than the sick, the pregnant, and young children, must fast in both body and mind from dawn until sunset.

Islam, which means submission to God, is the official religion of Qatar and it's the obligation of Muslims to abide by the five symbolic pillars.

The first pillar represents their allegiance to faith, and the second their commitment to prayer. A Muslim must face towards Mecca in Saudi Arabia, site of the oldest mono-theistic mosque, and pray five times a day; at dawn, midday, mid-afternoon, sunset and nightfall reciting the prescribed prayer:

> God is most great.
> I testify that
> there is no god but God
> and that Mohammad
> is the Prophet of God.

THE WASHING MACHINE WILL

Come to the prayer!
Come to the salvation!
God is most great.
There is no god but God.

These words are the first to be spoken to all newborn and the last to be delivered at death.

Qatar has around 800 mosques, 700 of them in Doha, and with probably no more than 225,000 Muslims, this gives a remarkable ratio of one mosque for every 280 prospective worshippers. A simple comparison with London would mean around 21,000 churches in the capital. And no bad thing. Less room for Asda stores.

Religion is fundamental to Muslims, particularly so in Qatar and Saudi Arabia, and forms an integral part of daily life. Five prayer sessions every day testify to this. Although my own lifestyle in Britain has hardly been a carousel of religious activity, this dedication in others gives the subject an odd compulsion.

With 1,000 million followers, Islam is the second largest religion after Christianity. It was established in the early 7th century when the spoken word of God was revealed to Mohammad in a cave near Mecca. These revelations became the Koran, a doctrine of meticulous detail by which its followers must live. Unlike Christianity, Islam isn't a private religion of personal conscience and ethics, rather a complete way of life encompassing the law, politics, health, domestic and social affairs. Muslims don't consider it to be an original religion. Merely a perceived correction of Christianity and Judaism, and although it recognises Christ as a holy figure of significance, it doesn't consider him to be The Son Of God.

So in Qatar religion comes first and is treated at all levels with appropriate esteem, from the state, which interrupts television and radio transmissions each day during the five calls to prayer, to the ordinary Muslim who, if unable to reach a mosque at the applicable time, will pray anyway. The daily spectacle of buses and cars discharging their passengers on the Doha–Umm Said highway at prayer times so they may kneel and face Mecca, its direction established from the sun, never loses its fascination to an infidel like myself. Doubtless only moments before, the same vehicles had overtaken me at unimaginable speed. Yet their passengers were now in quiet contemplation before, oblivious to the paradox, they once more resume their death-defying progress in the direction of the next prayer session. There must be a great solace to be gathered from such consummate belief in one's God.

Should access to a mosque prove impracticable, alternatives are readily to hand. Most offices have a communal prayer room, and many are the times when the discharging of vessels at the port ceases abruptly as the stevedores are called to prayer, their kneeling-mats unfurled on the ground like a Cairo bazaar.

On the highway between Doha and Umm Said is Al-Wakrah, the site of an old palace in the desert where some years ago a magnificent mosque was built. Floodlit each evening, to approach from a distance as it glows and quivers from the blackness like a floating mirage until proximity gives it precise definition, is quite one of the most stimulating tableaux imaginable – worthy of what it represents. And to see it framed by a desert sunset is no less imposing. I'm no enthusiast of architecture and frankly have yet to see a building anywhere in the world of more than mere transient interest. But the mosque at Al-Wakrah is an exception. Whether the interior is as impressive must remain unknown, to me at least. Only Muslims are permitted to enter mosques in Qatar. Which is a shame.

The third of the five symbolic pillars represents the obligatory charitable tax levied annually on the head of each family at a minimum of two and a half per cent of cash and property wealth. This is used to benefit deprived people.

THE WASHING MACHINE WILL

The fourth pillar is the fast – Ramadan – and the fifth the Hajj, a pilgrimage to Mecca which every Muslim who is medically able should make once in his or her lifetime. Around 2–3 million pilgrims a year make the journey to Mecca which, together with Medina, also in Saudi Arabia, is a holy city which may only be entered by Muslims. The significance of both places originates with the establishment of Islam in the early 7th century when Mohammad declared a Jihad, holy war, on pagan Mecca from where a few years before he'd migrated to live in Medina. Having assembled an army of 10,000 Arabs, huge in those times, he marched on Mecca, overwhelming the city. This subsequently led to a rapid conversion to Islam throughout the Middle East.

But today, and for the next four weeks, Ramadan dominates Qatar. Its purpose is to instil piety and self-restraint, and to demonstrate the suffering endured by the millions of starving people around the world who live a compulsory fast. Each morning at dawn, a cannon will sound to signify abstinence from food, drink and smoking until the dusk cannon indicates the overnight respite. We non-Muslims are forbidden to eat, drink, or smoke in public during the corresponding periods and to assist us in this task, all restaurants and food or drink retailers must remain closed within fasting times.

In around thirty days Ramadan ends, as it started, with the appearance of the new moon which is followed by the three-day Eid Festival of communal celebration in homes and streets. For Muslims, the Eid has a significance similar to Christmas for Christians. And after thirty days of fasting they'll have earned their right to a few days' excitement.

The moon is pivotal to Islam, with the year based not on the Gregorian, but the Hijra calendar. This comprises twelve lunar months of alternately twenty-nine or thirty days giving 354 days in each year. Hence, new year falls eleven days earlier each time moving backwards through the seasons in a thirty-two and a half year cycle. The start of the calendar corresponds to AD 622, the time Mohammad migrated from the corruption of Mecca to convert Medina to Islam. This Ramadan marks the start of the ninth month of the year 1412.

Last evening I spent with Mr Al-Khalifi. We discussed Islamic philosophy and he proposed I observe the fast, and if I maintain it successfully through until Eid, he will present me with a brass coffee-pot which has remained in his family for around forty years, and he's well aware I've coveted for months. He has also lent me an English-language copy of the Koran, a passage of which should be read each day during Ramadan.

Consequently, as from today I'm fasting, although my landlord is sceptical I'll see it through till the end. But what Mr Al-Khalifi doesn't know, and he doesn't know because I haven't told him, is that I rarely eat during the day anyway. My normal ill-advised routine is to take one substantial meal in the evening, then nothing for a further twenty-four hours. And I don't smoke. So not too much inconvenience so far. The lack of liquid will be the single obstacle. Not whilst in an office. Anyone should be capable of that for a month. But only time will reveal whether it creates an insurmountable hindrance to my outside work where frequent liquid intake is essential to maintain lost fluid levels and avoid dehydration. Although only spring, the temperatures are now approaching 100 Fahrenheit and I normally consume around 15 pints of water a day whilst working the ships at the port. But I want that coffee-pot.

* * * * *

Tim Manns came to the villa this evening and we shared a fourteen-egg omelette. If this sounds a trifle greedy, I should explain that Qatari eggs are considerably smaller than any others I've clapped eyes on. Using the British categorising system, you'd be lucky to find one that beats a twelve.

THE WASHING MACHINE WILL

I hadn't appreciated from our previous conversations just how many well-known people he's interviewed for Radio Bahrain, where the state's interpretation of Islamic principles is not as strict as in Qatar. Accordingly, some of the hotels regularly promote British acts which perform in a night-club environment. Not all the names were as instantly recognisable to me as they were to Tim, but nevertheless the list was noteworthy as immediately they arrived in Bahrain, the acts would hotfoot over to his programme to promote their shows.

Tommy Cooper, Billy Connolly, Frankie Howerd, Jasper Carrott, Rowan Atkinson, Gary Glitter are but a modest selection, whilst most illustrious of all was Status Quo. Mr Manns' prestige promptly shot skywards in my estimation when he told me. Not everyone, I appreciate, may share that view.

Quo visited Bahrain in 1986 to appear at a local hotel – their first performance since opening the Wembley Live Aid concert the previous year. Can Live Aid really be almost seven years ago?

But there was one question I had to ask. Although the State of Bahrain is more indulgent in its judgment of the permitted level of perceived Western decadence than Qatar, it's still an Arab country. And there is a limit to everything. So how did you fare with Billy Connolly? was the unavoidable question.

Acknowledging his normally risqué public performances, before the broadcast Tim had explained to Billy there were six subjects which should not be mentioned on the radio, namely sex, politics, religion, alcohol, drugs and smoking. He nodded, and the interview, which was scheduled to last thirty minutes, began.

'Good afternoon, everyone. Today we are pleased to have with us Billy Connolly who arrived from London this morning. Welcome, Billy.'

'Thanks, Tim. But before we start, I just heard a great joke on the aircraft. There was this chainsmoking, Muslim politician who was caught drunk in a drugs raid on a sex club in Amsterdam.'

Tim was just lunging for the microphone control to cut the sound, when Billy collapsed in hysterics before performing with exemplary decorum for the remainder of the interview.

The omelette was awful.

✳ ✳ ✳ ✳ ✳

Our local post-office has recently started flogging live chickens along with the stamps and blue airmails. And what an excellent wheeze this is. Diversification is the means to profitability in these days of economic gloom. A lesson there for British post-offices perhaps.

Of course, given the average length of the queue at a British post-office, it's likely the chickens would be more dead than alive by the time you'd reached the front. And on reflection, there are better ways of spending your unemployment benefit these days than harbouring a horde of chickens. So best forget it.

To advertise this innovation, the proprietor of our post-office has both painted in green, and slightly mis-spelled, a large sign on his window stating, 'Relieble Live Chickens'. Ignoring the question of how in heaven's name any chicken could possibly be described as reliable, there's ironic significance in the mis-spelling of this word as reliability is not one of the pre-eminent characteristics of life in Qatar. Example coming up.

Two weeks ago I was sitting quietly in my lounge darning a sock. Without warning there was a crash from the bathroom of such intensity both cats shot three feet in the air before landing with their fur rigid, their backs arched and their tails pointing straight to the heavens. I knew how they felt. To be strictly accurate, only Scarface 1 had his tail thrust skywards as only Scarface 1 has a tail. Scarface 2 merely aimed his stump in a vaguely vertical direction. It was a week before the poor things fully recovered either their equilibrium or appetites and I still need to play them soft, soothing music some evenings. They like Des O'Connor. Pity. Such was the commotion even the goats refrained from their usual irritating interference and scooted off due south for the remainder of the day.

But by now, I imagine you must be either frantic with worry as to the cause of this disturbance in the bathroom, or fast asleep. Assuming it to be the former, I can disclose prompt investigation revealed the sink had collapsed from the wall and smashed on the stone floor into numerous pieces, raising serious questions as to its continuing serviceability.

Qatar, of course, is not an ideal place to be lacking a reliable sink. Consequently, I telephoned the maintenance supervisor at Mr Al-Khalifi's office to outline the circumstances, and received immediate and confident reassurance.

'No problem, Mr Peter. I get replacement sink and fit anytime.'

'OK. How about today?'

'No, today impossible. Sorry.'

'OK. How about tomorrow?'

'No, tomorrow impossible. Sorry.'

'OK. How about the day after?'

'No, day after impossible. Sorry.'

'OK. How about I come round to your office and kill you? Would Tuesday be possible?'

Laughing a touch apprehensively, he promised the matter would receive the priority attention of himself and what appeared to be practically everyone else in Qatar. But I wasn't so sure. By the time it turns up, I thought, I'll either be past caring or dead. Probably both.

It was nearly two weeks before the new sink arrived. As did a second twenty minutes later. On phoning the supervisor to enquire why I was now being inundated with sinks, he directed me to select which colour I preferred, a comparatively simple exercise as they were identical. Concerning the delay, the man explained it resulted from a necessity to import them both from Dubai. This particular type was apparently uncommon and, excluding mine, only five others were fitted in the whole of Qatar. By coincidence, as I've been going about my daily routine in Doha this week, I've spotted eighteen of those five sinks.

So a word of warning. As far as reliability is concerned, I recommend you show considerable caution before believing everything anyone tells you. And you can trust me. I'm relieble.

A complication arose on the first occasion I used the immigrant sink and its cause wasn't difficult to establish. It was the plug. It didn't have one. So rather than wait two centuries while the maintenance man scoured the Middle East, I meandered along to the local hardware shop.

'One sink plug, please.'

'Yes, what size?'

'Normal, please.'

'No problem. All same size. No charge.'

What a nice man.

On returning to the villa, it was soon apparent Qatari sink plugs don't necessarily conform to international standards. Having spent twenty minutes attempting to retrieve the blasted thing from down the plug-hole, and then a further fifteen grappling with the plastic ruler employed in an unsuccessful salvage operation before it too became irretrievably lost, I gave up and after meticulously measuring the gap trudged back to the store.

Despite the storekeeper's personal guarantee as to its dependability, this time the replacement plug proved marginally too large. Which is why, if you happened to be in Doha the other day, you may have spotted me lurching along the road with a sink under my arm. It seemed the only way to resolve this lamentable affair was with a personal fitting. It worked. But then one thing led to another.

No sooner had the plug-hole nuisance been eliminated and the sink re-fitted, than the hassle returned. This time it was the tap. I could hear it from the kitchen. Drip. Drip. Drip. Drip. Drip. Tightening proved ineffective so I plumped instead for indifference.

Drip. Drip. Drip. Drip. Drip. The cats were becoming mesmerized as they crouched on the edge of the bath, their eyes – or in the case of Scarface 2, eye – following each droplet into the sink.

In the kitchen, I was diligently sorting a selection of horse bones. They were unexpectedly donated from next door for the goats, initially I'd assumed for their nourishment, but on reflection maybe they're for beating the living daylights out of them. But the persistence of the tap soon became intolerable. Drip. Drip. Drip. Drip. Drip.

Liberating the cats from their trance with a single click of my fingers, and gripping the transgressing tap with a pair of pliers, I gave it a single, determined twist. As I explained to the men from the Water Department as they pumped out the villa, they don't make taps like in the old days.

After reporting this nonsense to Mr Al-Khalifi and having been reminded of my liabilities in respect of wilful damage, he proposed I organise any necessary redecoration at my own expense not only, I suspect, as it was technically my fault, but because his own maintenance staff were fully committed in rebuilding a flat they'd blown up the previous week. I know that for a fact. Moira told me.

It didn't take long to decide who to invite to effect the appropriate restoration in the bathroom. Whether the work was strictly necessary is a matter for conjecture as frankly it was probably cleaner after the tap skirmish than it had been for years. But what the hell.

Driving through Doha recently, I'd been interested to observe that my old friend Vincent, half-man half-sneeze,

has started a decorating and home repairs business operating from tiny premises near the airport. Just scrambling
inside must be proving a struggle given his generous
frame. I didn't stop, but observed him through the window
blowing his nose whilst attaching a notice to the door
which read 'No job too small'. A couple of hours later I
phoned from home and asked him to come round to
unwrap a choc-ice. He thought that hugely amusing. So
did I at the time.

However, on this second occasion, the purpose of my call
was genuine, to procure his services to redecorate my
bathroom, and it was agreed work would commence the
following day.

'Pale blue emulsion will look good, Vincent. Don't forget
to bring.'

The following day arrived but Vincent didn't. His van
jammed in first gear. Then the mobile mechanic organised
to remedy the defect collided with a camel and was diverted
to hospital. Fortunately the camel, if it existed, was unhurt.
I've no news of the mechanic.

It was the next day work began, which was yesterday.
Vincent arrived in good health, together with three large tins
of emulsion, an impressive array of brushes and a pair of
gleaming white overalls with 'Vincent – The Best' em-
blazoned across the back. That's my boy! He immediately
set to work, neatly removing the lid from one of the tins with
a fork. Oh, dear!

'This paint is pale green, Vincent. I said pale blue.'

'No, definite pale blue. Says so on tin.'

'Yes. I see tin says blue, but paint inside is green.'

Never one to be easily unsettled by events, or indeed
instructions, Vincent began painting the bathroom. It was to
be green.

As he's an inveterate tea drinker, by early evening my
milk supply was exhausted. Using his van, we drove to the
local store and leaving Vincent waiting in the car park, I

vanished inside. Minutes later, I emerged with eight cartons of milk in a plastic bag, placed it on the ground and waved to Vincent. Reversing from the car park at breakneck speed, he ploughed straight into the shopping, splitting the cartons and leaving me with a plastic bag containing eight pints of swirling milk. Idiot. Back inside the shop, I handed the bag to the assistant and collected eight further cartons. He looked puzzled.

'What happened, Mr Peter?'

'Vincent.'

'I understand.'

As we returned to the villa, Vincent was profuse in his apologies, saying a special prayer of atonement. I should think so. And also for that 'my other car is a camel' sticker on his rear window.

It was an hour later the commotion began. What appears to have happened is Vincent took a discreet cigarette break. Then, discovering the paint tin had stuck resolutely to the floor, the vigorous tug intended to loosen it had all but drowned one of the cats which, as a result, was overcome with emulsion. It proved to be Scarface 2 – not that identification was immediately possible. The poor thing completely lost its mind, not only due to this unexpected refurbishment, but at the disconcerting spectacle of innumerable pale green pawprints chasing it around the villa. Later that evening, his mood became so distressed he attempted suicide by throwing himself under the vacuum cleaner. But the cleaner came off worse.

On reflection, the bathroom looks good in green.

❋ ❋ ❋ ❋ ❋

Every Friday morning, the English service of Qatar Radio transmits an hour-long programme when children can telephone the studio and talk on air to request records.

For many years this programme has been hosted by an

IF THE SUN DOESN'T KILL YOU,

Irish lady known to one and all as Aunty Lucy, and she's very popular with the children, and with me too, since I heard her tell listeners about some Egyptian onions she'd been chopping at home which proved especially strong. So much so that while she peeled them in Doha, half of Dublin collapsed in tears. She's an offbeat character is Aunty Lucy. All the rooms in her home have been allotted their own Christian names, the two toilets being called Elton and Olivia Newton. But let's get to the point.

Last Friday I was listening to Aunty Lucy whilst vacuum cleaning the goats. She was speaking about William and Harry, the children of Prince Charles and Princess Diana, and how they are given expensive presents on their birthdays – not primarily by their parents, but by private organisations and individuals.

Aunty Lucy read an extract from an article in which some British children had been questioned as to what birthday presents they would like if they could choose anything they wanted. And I recall one boy asked to be given Concorde so he could fly anywhere in the world. Another craved his own recording studio so he could meet Madonna, and a girl wanted to own the biggest diamond in the world.

A few minutes later, a nine-year-old Bangladeshi girl called Jasmine telephoned Aunty Lucy from her home on the Paradise Estate in Umm Said. This incongruously named estate is a particularly squalid block of residences, inhabited mainly by manual workers and their families who are very much at the lower end of the social structure here and live in conditions you or I would find quite unacceptable.

Aunty Lucy asked Jasmine if the Fairy Queen could bring her any present regardless of cost, what would she like most in the world. The little girl thought for a moment then said,

'What I've always wanted more than anything else is a jigsaw puzzle.'

Now doesn't an answer like that make you think? It says more about the inequality of life than any political rhetoric could ever do. To that little girl the unattainable was a jigsaw puzzle. And yet to most children in Britain, such a present would warrant scant attention before being thrown into a drawer to be dismissed for the far greater delights of computer games, bicycles, videos and numerous other expensive attractions.

Whilst Qatar isn't exactly a Shangri-La on earth, it can certainly provide a fair old perspective of life.

* * * * *

It's Eid. It's a holiday. And I collected that coffee-pot from Mr Al-Khalifi this evening.

My daytime abstinence from liquid during Ramadan proved demanding – as indeed it should. But I was fortunate. A dearth of incoming ships during the period, together with the much curtailed working hours, resulted in fewer outside activities than usual. And the temperature was kind to us, being abnormally low during the month. And the Koran proved strangely edifying.

Moira cooked a simple but fine meal tonight. I don't normally get involved in recipes, although a dashed fine cook myself. But on this occasion I'll make an exception.

Cook skinned chicken breasts immersed in a mixture for each person of:

1 x 330 ml can of 7UP.
1 tablespoon of soy sauce.
1 tablespoon of concentrated lemon juice.
2 level teaspoons of sugar.
2 level tablespoons of cornflower.
Add chopped onions, mushrooms, sliced pineapple, and sultanas.

Delicious. I had mine with chips and peas. Moira does great chips for an Australian.

*

This afternoon the three of us visited the camel racing track situated in the desert twelve miles outside Doha, as Mr Al-Khalifi had one of his camels entered in the main event. The U-shaped course of compacted sand is about three times wider than a standard British horse-racing track and five miles in length. But Royal Ascot it isn't.

As we arrived, preparations seemed well under way. At the starting point around fifty camels were being marshalled by an Indian with a huge crimson flag into something vaguely reminiscent of a line. Less than half appeared to be facing the prescribed direction and three weren't even standing. Each one was mounted by a tiny Indian boy of eight or nine years old, Velcroed precariously on to the saddle. By the age of ten, most jockeys are considered too grown to race and must then retire.

Although Mr Al-Khalifi remained with Moira and myself in the grandstand, the majority of owners, who were competing for a Mercedes car, assembled in four-wheel drive jeeps by the rails at each side of the track. The instant the tape flew upwards, the cavalcade shot off amid a deafening roar to pursue their beasts around the course.

Confronted with this unexpected commotion, for the first ten seconds the alarmed camels ran in all directions, provoking a series of ungainly collisions. It only needed a policeman with a whistle and it was the driving test all over again. What transpired after the first ten seconds was impossible to establish as by that stage the entire extravaganza became enveloped in a vast cloud of sand and dust generated by the accelerating jeeps. By the time visibility had been restored, most of the camels had vacated the immediate area – with the exception of number seven which was either asleep or dead on the starting line. It's not always easy to tell with camels.

Half an hour later an approaching cloud the size of Norway indicated the leaders were about to reach the finish. With the assistance of Mr Al-Khalifi's binoculars, it was just possible to distinguish them as they passed the winning post. First was a Range Rover followed by two Suzukis.

Two minutes later, around a dozen uninterested-looking camels ambled through to the finish. They were brought unceremoniously to a halt by a barricade of jeeps strung across the track for the purpose. We never spotted Mr Al-Khalifi's entry although he didn't seem too bothered. Nor would I have been.

This was probably my first and last excursion into the world of camel racing. It was all too reminiscent of the Doha ring road on a Friday night. I was all but involved in an accident on the way home this evening at one of the roundabouts. The fact it's best to go round them still seems to cause people confusion.

✳ ✳ ✳ ✳ ✳

It's the general election in the United Kingdom tomorrow. Tim informs me a new BBC World Television Service which can be received in Bahrain will transmit its domestic election night results programme hosted by David Dimbleby. Politics being a passion of mine, I've decided to fly to Bahrain for twenty-four hours to watch the proceedings from a hotel.

Being so distant from the campaign during recent weeks has proved frustrating, and to receive an objective view Tim and I have clubbed together to buy *The Times* newspaper each day – the political impartiality of my more usual *Daily Mail* being subject to doubt. *The Times* costs the equivalent of four pounds here but has been good value. Not that I'd plough through it *every* day in normal circumstances.

Regrettably, I'll not be voting for anyone. Some weeks ago I completed and posted to London an application form available from the British Embassy which requested authority for a postal vote. The volume of information solicited was unimaginable and, as best I recall, most of the questions seemed utterly irrelevant. How long have you lived abroad? What is your address in the United Kingdom? Have you ever owned a swivel chair? Did you write on your ruler at school? Do you talk to your pet in a silly voice when there's no one around? Is it true what they say about Dixie? Ridiculous! Why do they need all this stuff just for a postal vote? Presumably I didn't answer the questions correctly as I've heard nothing since. Pity. Screaming Lord Sutch needs every vote he can get.

Tim and I have made a wager on the outcome. He thinks Major will win and I've given him odds of two to one based on fifty riyals. Whoever loses gives the money to the local Sudan fund. The reports from there on Qatar television are dreadful to watch. As of today, it seems Kinnock will finally make it, or so the opinion poll in *The Times* indicates. He's waited long enough. But then I recall Arsenal leading against Luton in the last few minutes of the League Cup Final at Wembley – and still contriving to lose. I was so upset.

10

Election special. Major saves his bacon. Read all about it.

I've just seen something most unexpected. After collecting my exit visa from the Immigration Office earlier today, this evening I visited Mr Al-Khalifi who wants me to take some mail to Bahrain. Standing in their kitchen, I glanced across to the spot where the rare, forty-year-old brass coffee-pot which is now in my possession had stood. And there to my astonishment was an identical pot. That Mr Al-Khalifi is a rascal.

I looked accusingly across at him. And he smiled benignly back at me.

'Never mind. You got what you wanted. And always remember – life is what you make it.'

I must have appeared surprised at hearing this very Western cliché.

'It's from a well-known Arab fable,' he explained, 'concerning three nomads who travelled into the desert in search of the great wise man. For six weeks they journeyed through the burning heat of day, only resting when the black veil of night fell helplessly to the ground.'

This is no well-known Arab fable, I thought. This is one of his jokes.

'Finally, after ten weeks, the nomads came to the abode of the wise man and were taken to his servant.

' "We have come to see the great wise man to learn the meaning of life," said the nomads.

' "Yes," came the reply. "But first you must spend a year in solemn meditation." '

No question. This is definitely a joke.

'After a year, the three nomads returned to the servant who took them into the presence of the wise man.

' "We have each meditated for a year, oh great wise man. Now will you tell us the meaning of life?"

'For ten minutes the man sat in deep contemplation. Finally he stood up and spoke.

' "Life," he said, slowly stretching his arms outwards before him, "is what you make it." And he walked majestically back to his quarters and closed the door.'

I knew it. An Al-Khalifi joke. In my experience, the exasperating characteristic of Arab jokes is that they differ from most others in one fundamental respect. They're not funny. And not only that, it's difficult to understand how they could have been funny even in their original Arabic. But then what would the Emir of Qatar, Sheikh Khalifa Bin-Hamad Al-Thani have made of Jasper Carrott? Not a lot, I suspect.

Leaving Mr Al-Khalifi, I drove home, but first visited Kylie to collect a Bob Seger tape she had borrowed from me some weeks ago. Not uncharacteristically it hadn't been returned. There are a number of essentials for living in Qatar and Bob Seger tapes is one of them. But I could have guessed what was coming. Kylie's style never varies.

'I've got good news and bad news.'

'So what's the bad news?'

'I've lost your tape.'

'And what's the good news?'

'It's my birthday tomorrow.'

I suddenly felt an all-consuming desire to fill her car windscreen washer bottle with Batchelors cream of chicken soup. That would give her something to think about next time she cleaned her screen. How can a country which gave us Olivia Newton-John be responsible for Kylie?

I hope she's not expecting a birthday card. I wonder if the lighthouse shop in Umm Said sells 'I'm sorry you're so irksome' cards?

✱ ✱ ✱ ✱ ✱

My brief election special to Bahrain proved singularly eventful even when judged against the standards of Qatar.

I stayed at the Al-Bustan, a capacious hotel in comparison to which Buckingham Palace assumes the significance of a Butlins chalet. I can only surmise it was built on the assumption half the world's population would arrive in Bahrain on the same day all looking for hotel accommodation.

I was in room 1602, which had a bathroom the size of a cathedral, a bath with the specifications of an Olympic pool, and sufficient towels to re-stock Selfridges. The room had three telephones and just to call reception required the assistance of the long-distance operator. OK, perhaps I'm exaggerating a little, but you get the picture.

In the basement of the hotel was a discotheque, a decadence not permitted in Qatar. And judging by the row emanating from the place last night, Qataris know a good thing when they can't hear it. Feeling trendy at the time, I descended into the cacophonous gloom and by an amazing coincidence met a friend called Brian Rosier who was visiting Bahrain on business. But the music was so deafening our attempts to communicate were manifestly unproductive and we only managed one of those ridiculous 'you said' conversations which are inclined to result in such adverse circumstances.

'I'm sorry, what was that you said?'

'I said I'm sorry I didn't catch what you said.'

'I said it's impossible to hear what anyone says.'

'I'm sorry, what was that you said?'

We left the discotheque to throb itself to death and, with three hours before the start of the election broadcast, Brian and I headed for the self-service restaurant.

Finding ourselves in a queue of around thirty people all waiting to pay the single cashier, our chicken nuggets and chips were rapidly turning cold. This left us with only one reasonable course of action. We ate them. Fifteen minutes later having finally arrived at the cash desk, the bemused man was confronted with two empty plates and a spoiled serviette. Failing to appreciate the logic of the situation, the cashier flapped extravagantly in the general direction of the manager who dashed across to establish the cause of the disturbance. It was a further five minutes before our innocent intentions were acknowledged, by which time the queue stretched twice around the restaurant.

The next two hours we spent in the lounge engaged in jovial reminiscence, whilst subject to the reproving eye of the manager who made regular sorties in our direction to ensure we were behaving ourselves.

I've known Brian for years and he's one of the most discernibly honest people I've met. If a man smashed his way into a National Westminster Bank with a sawn-off shotgun and yelled 'Everyone hit the deck', Brian Rosier would not be that man. In the late seventies, he came for a job interview at the company where I worked. An hour after the scheduled start I checked with the personnel manager to establish how things had gone, only to be advised the meeting hadn't started. It seemed Brian had somehow got caught up in someone else's fire drill for three-quarters of an hour. He got the job, but now operates his own road transport, distribution and warehousing company in Harlow which is performing impressively even during the current recession. When launching it with just one lorry in 1986, Brian invited my opinion as to a suitable trading name. After lengthy deliberation I offered a number of particularly creative suggestions. He then chose Rosier Transport which shows his opinion of my ideas.

The company now operates in excess of 200 vehicles, with 300 employees at various depots in both Britain and France and recently received some sort of British Standards award for being wonderful – which demonstrates what hard graft can achieve. No one ever gave me an award.

Since our last meeting twelve months ago, Brian has become involved in the chemical industry and bought himself a factory. It's in Birmingham. So it would easily fit inside my television. He not only distributes the stuff, but refines base chemicals before manufacturing a variety of allied products mostly with names of at least forty letters which would need Anna Ford to pronounce.

We took the lift to my room on the sixteenth floor stopping only to collect an oxygen cylinder from reception. There I go exaggerating again. With an hour to wait before the election transmission, we decided to discover what delights the Bahraini television service had to offer two international businessmen like ourselves.

The television stood on a veneered shelf which was connected to the wall by a metal frame the proportions of which rivalled the Forth Bridge. OK. No more I promise.

We settled down to watch *Give Us A Clue* dubbed into Arabic, which seemed an improvement on *Give Us A Clue* transmitted in English. However, no sooner had Lionel Blair begun miming, 'I'm Dreaming Of A White Christmas', than the shelf and television shuddered momentarily before the frame parted company from its moorings, resulting in all three plunging noisily to the floor. The impact wrecked much of the surrounding area and the ensuing debris was soon joined by a substantial chunk of what had previously been the wall. The small fire which then followed was quickly extinguished by both our presence of mind and a bottle of Pepsi-Cola. So disconcerting was all this, I suddenly recalled why I've never been over-keen on Lionel Blair. What luck. First my sink, and now this.

You'll be relieved to learn, the management of the hotel subsequently absolved us of all responsibility for this regrettable incident – as they confirmed when we handed in both halves of the fridge door handle.

We returned to the television lounge to watch the election results as everyone thought it safer. And Kinnock lost again. So much for my astute prediction, and my 100 riyals. The programme was compulsive and I watched through to its conclusion nine hours later by which time Brian had long since capitulated to his early morning flight back to London. To collect another award no doubt. But it was good to see him again. Only time will tell if the same applies to John Major.

Arriving back at Doha Airport this afternoon, I was promptly arrested and detained in the police room for more than an hour. It was my own fault. I'm fully aware the importation of bacon into Qatar is banned. The Koran forbids the consumption of meat from the pig as it's considered an unclean animal. Of course some may believe the poor things to be no grubbier than a number of other animals. But on solely practical grounds the decree is well-founded as the pig has both a high fat content, and in excessive temperatures is more readily susceptible to disease, trichinosis for example, than other animals. But being a devotee of bacon I decided the mouthwatering benefit would merit the risk.

It was only six rashers which I'd bought in the hotel store in Bahrain where no such restriction applies. The pack was slipped out of sight between a wad of papers inside my briefcase, although not sufficiently concealed to give a positive impression of deliberate intent.

The police discovered the bacon immediately and I was

whisked off to the interview room to profess utter amazement at learning of its restriction.

'As it was OK with your brothers in Bahrain, officer, I assumed it was good for Qatar.'

After a barrage of questions I was released, although the bacon detained for further interrogation.

I had a meal of eggs and chips this evening. Had it been supplemented by those rashers it would have been delicious. I wonder what the police officer from the Bacon Squad had for his tea? But it was a stupid move and I'm saying nothing further without my solicitor.

This bacon swoop wasn't the only excitement at the airport this afternoon as the Emir of Qatar was returning from a goodwill visit to Egypt. According to today's *Gulf Times*, whilst there he was taken for a tour of a city called 10th of Ramadan. The 10th of Ramadan, of course, is a date in the Muslim Hijrah calendar and it's an interesting notion to call towns or cities after dates. And one that's laden with potential.

Imagine if Britain adopted this policy. You could enter the booking hall at Euston Station, approach the ticket desk and say, 'Excuse me. I'd like to buy a cheap day return to 27 November, please.'

Or what about the football results?

Arsenal 1 – 22 February 1, after extra time. The replay will be at 22 February on the 23 February.

Or can you visualise the motorway road works information?

Delays at the junction 12 turn-off for 8 May, will occur between 7 May and 9 May. Follow signposted diversions via 5 August.

I can see very interesting possibilities in this and propose we now finish with an appropriate sing-song.

We could start with 'Maybe It's Because I'm A 23 Apriler'.

Then into 'I Belong To 30 November'. And finally 'It's A Long Way To 17 March'. You can't beat the good old favourites. The words really mean something.

I've just been listening on the BBC World Service, to most of a speech John Major gave outside 10 Downing Street today following his victory. In it he declared that during the past decade the quality of life in the United Kingdom has improved significantly for us all. That's a fascinating assessment. I can't help wondering when Mr Major last travelled on the Northern Line during the rush hour, or tried to get a hospital appointment in under six years, or watched *The Word* on Channel Four. Just a thought.

11
Two slender ladies and a doughnut.

My cooker has temporarily withdrawn its co-operation. I say temporarily, as Mr Al-Khalifi's maintenance man has promised to visit the villa tomorrow to administer the appropriate repairs, which, from previous experience, will mean clobbering it with a sledgehammer. Precluded therefore from experiencing the delights of home-cooking, earlier this evening I drove to the pizza take-away restaurant – that sanctuary for an international businessman like myself. However, a most curious sequence of incidents occurred.

During my journey, on at least half a dozen occasions, other drivers flashed their headlights or waved at me. Arriving at the restaurant around seven o'clock, I found it shut, with a 'Gone to Lunch' sign in the window. But why had so many people been trying to attract my attention? I checked the tyres, the exhaust, all the doors. But nothing. And on my return journey precisely the same thing happened. Headlights flashing. Arms waving. I was mystified.

Back at the villa, I methodically rechecked the car but again found no indication as to the cause of all the concern. And then suddenly it dawned on me. I'd forgotten to iron my shirt.

IF THE SUN DOESN'T KILL YOU,

Now I appreciate you may find this episode difficult to believe. And if so you'd be right. It was a complete lie I told my landlord as retribution for the great wise man fable. I'm not certain if he believed me. You can never tell with Mr Al-Khalifi. He has an Australian wife, you know.

✳ ✳ ✳ ✳ ✳

Six hours ago I saw a young Arab boy drown. It's now midnight and not easy to rationalise my feelings. The cliché is to express both shock at witnessing this tragedy and distress at the anguish which has befallen the boy's distraught parents. They were also present.

But if I'm honest I feel nothing. Not specifically concerning the fact – just nothing. I feel the sympathy, but there's no emotion. And I don't understand why. It's like waking abruptly during the night after watching a profoundly realistic film shortly before sleeping. In such circumstances, the disorientated mind is often unable to instantly differentiate between fact and fiction. Was it a news bulletin or a film I was watching? And it can take some seconds to distinguish the truth. At the moment I'm having difficulty in recognising the reality. But that's what it is.

I'd been sitting reading earlier this evening in the otherwise unoccupied garden of a private residential complex in Doha, awaiting the arrival of a friend. A swimming pool was about fifty yards away. Save for a middle-aged Arab man it was deserted, although a few minutes previously it had been noisily appreciated by about a dozen young children who had since been reluctantly persuaded away by their single supervising adult.

My reading was interrupted by an abrupt shout from the swimmer. As I glanced towards the pool he had already dived beneath the water. With no initial appreciation of anything untoward, indeed I was not even certain it was the swimmer who had called, my eye remained idly on the water awaiting his re-emergence. Within seconds the man surfaced, dragging what transpired to be the boy, although from my position this was not immediately evident. Reaching the side of the pool he made a brief abortive attempt to ascend the steps. Looking around he saw me, and after a summoning wave, shouted something in Arabic. I walked and, sensing urgency, then ran to the pool.

The man pushed the boy upwards towards me and I hauled him on to the poolside, his inordinate weight as a consequence of water inhalation, taking me by surprise. His bloated, anaemic appearance was a shock that will be understood by anyone with the misfortune to have experienced similar circumstances.

Pulling himself from the water, the man instructed me to telephone the local hospital, reciting the number from memory. By an opportune, but ultimately ineffectual coincidence, he was a paediatrician, and by the time I'd returned after calling an ambulance, had begun mouth-to-mouth resuscitation. The boy, who must have been lying at the bottom of the pool for at least five minutes, wasn't breathing although the doctor had detected a weak pulse.

For ten minutes he continued to alternately beat the boy's chest and blow into his throat, ignoring the vomit simultaneously exuding into and over himself.

At this juncture, wisely or not, someone brought the boy's parents to the scene. It would be intrusive to detail their reaction, suffice to recount both required medical attention. Thankfully, by now the ambulance had arrived, its assistance welcome to the overburdened doctor.

A tube was inserted into the boy's throat and the doctor continued working. By this time no pulse had been detected for more than five minutes and the doctor's frustration at the futility of his efforts was becoming evident, as was his fatigue. The boy's body was removed in the ambulance after a further fifteen minutes accompanied by the doctor, himself looking in need of attention.

119

IF THE SUN DOESN'T KILL YOU,

I'm uncertain why I've related this ordeal. Shocking as it was, and it will be an abiding memory, I suspect my purpose is to acknowledge the resolute devotion of a doctor to his job. For so many of us, a doctor at work is symbolised by someone sitting in a comfortable surgery tapping out prescriptions on a computer. For the most part, thank God, we don't see the rest.

The boy was Sudanese and his name was Jamal. He was four years old. One more tragedy for that wretched country. But countries, of course, don't grieve. Just parents.

✳ ✳ ✳ ✳ ✳

My neighbour has complained to Mr Al-Khalifi concerning the goats. It seems they've eaten his garage. Some people beef about anything these days. Yes, I can recognise the convenience of having an uneaten garage, but candidly, with his car too gigantic to get in, he only boarded an old boat, half a dozen chickens and a rasping cockerel in there. It was doubtless the latter the goats were after. Not that I harbour an excess of sympathy for the cockerel which frequently keeps me awake half the night with its interminable racket and was the prime cause of my nodding off at the airport lights a while back. It's meant to be a dawn chorus – so why can't the blasted bird learn to tell the time?

My landlord's placatory attempts apparently proved futile and he suggested a session between us to review matters could be of value, which explains my presence in his office this morning.

It was early in our deliberations that we conceded there was little to be done in respect of the goats and consequently broadened our terms of reference. We were discussing current world issues, the role of the United Nations in Middle East politics, the price of strawberries at Wimbledon, that sort of thing, when Mr Al-Khalifi suddenly produced a packet of dejected-looking sandwiches and began eating them.

This rather startled me as you don't expect someone who can afford fifteen fatted calves to be on call whenever he's feeling a bit peckish, to whip out a packet of sandwiches and start eating them in the middle of a conversation about world affairs. Obviously noticing my puzzled expression, he asked if I'd like one.

'Thank you very much,' I fawned, as it's considered impolite in the Arab world to decline such an offer. 'What's in it?'

'Cheese and jam.'

Oh, no. Not cheese and jam, I thought. Why can't he eat egg and tomato like anyone else?

Accepting the sandwich, sure enough, it was cheddar cheese and strawberry jam, and I was just wondering how on earth to cope with this atrocious concoction when a stroke of good fortune showed up. From the minarets of various nearby mosques echoed the midday call to prayers. And mine were answered as Mr Al-Khalifi swept away at breakneck speed for a quick pray.

Thankfully reprieved from eating this appalling sandwich, I slipped it surreptitiously into my briefcase, later consigning it to the most appropriate place that came to mind – namely down the throat of one of the goats. In fact the four of them had a fight over it. On reflection, I'm glad I'm not a goat.

But my reprieve was short-lived. Until this afternoon in fact, when visiting the Port at Umm Said.

As the working hours for the stevedores are long, and in arduous conditions, it's standard practice for the Port Authority to allow them a break during the day when rolls together with water are delivered to the men for their refreshment. On this occasion, the foreman of the stevedores, noting what he presumably considered to be my emaciated-looking appearance, kindly offered me one of the supply of rolls which they were all devouring with great fervour. Having examined the roll which I identified as processed cheese and pickle, and not wishing to give even a hint of offence, I graciously accepted his offer. I then re-checked it to ensure there was nothing moving inside, took an enormous bite – and you've guessed it. It wasn't cheese and pickle at all. It was cheese and marmalade. Absolutely bloody awful it was.

Now I'm no lover of marmalade at the best of times. Come to think of it, I don't go much on cheese either. And rolls have always struck me as rather dry and plasticky tasting. So why I agreed to eat the thing in the first place I can't imagine. But cheese and marmalade! And yet all the stevedores were quite happily munching away. Apparently it's considered quite normal here to mix cheese with jams and they were greatly amused at my reluctance to share their enjoyment. All of which rather left me with egg on my face. Or at least processed cheese and marmalade.

Which just about wraps the subject up as, apart from one of the port workers reversing a fork-lift truck off the quay into 30 feet of water, that was the most exciting thing to happen today. Which just shows the average day in Qatar is much the same here as anywhere else. Probably.

As the only decisive consequence of this morning's dialogue with Mr Al-Khalifi, I've returned to the villa this evening with three further tins of mutton and goat pie. Perhaps dispensing them around the courtyard to indicate there's more than one viable method of keeping goats, could prove effective. At this stage anything's worth trying.

✳ ✳ ✳ ✳ ✳

You're never far from the unexpected in Qatar. Last evening I gave a brilliant speech to sixty people at a farewell dinner for the manager of a transport company in Doha. No one told me until later that apart from myself, only one other person in attendance was able to speak more than two words of English. And if the bemused expressions on the

122

faces of my audience was any indication, the second of those was 'off'.

No sooner had I completed my speech than the cook appeared from the baker's next door and presented me with an enormous cake wishing me 'Bon voyage' in mauve icing. Which brings me to the display signs in shop windows. You can usually rely on them for the unexpected.

For discussion purposes, let's assume you called into Marks & Spencer this morning and there was a sign on the door which advised, 'We regret we were open yesterday', or at Tesco you saw a notice pleading, 'Please like us in future', then I suspect you'd find shopping a good deal more interesting than usual. We get plenty of this type of entertainment in Qatar, the signs in shop windows being a constant source of wonder and confusion.

'Please mind your head due to hole' and 'We want you to go without purchase', are two typical examples I've spotted today, whilst the significance of a sign in the window of a clothes shop near the Doha Souq which read 'Don't leave us', is slightly less evident.

But no such ambiguity seemed to prevail when I passed my favourite shop in Doha this evening which sells the cheap cassette tapes. On the window was a very specific sign which stated, 'You ask for it, we have got it'. So you see this red rag?

Inside the shop, the proprietor Mr Memnon Menon proved to be absent, but his assistant lurked furtively in a corner, munching a hard-boiled egg. He waved in greeting and then in the general direction of a wooden seat, the back of which lay in three pieces beside the counter. Producing a tin mug from an enormous carrier bag, he blew out a cloud of dust and poured a generous measure of sweet-smelling tea from a hip flask. Little more than fifty per cent made it into the mug. Pushing it along the counter towards me, he used such ferocity that all but a spoonful sloshed on to the floor. Moments later, a hard-boiled egg rolled erratically in my direction. Presumably compensation.

The man's imaginative use of the English language proved most endearing, blending the rudimentary with the sophisticated.

'Hello, pleese. Go look. Best shop Doha. Incomparable discounts negotiable.'

I surveyed the racks of cassette tapes. To begin, I thought, I'll start with a couple of easy ones to see how we progress.

'Good evening. I'd like to buy some cassette tapes please,' and pointed to the sign on the window. 'Do you have Madonna's *Greatest Hits*?'

The man shook his head vigorously and gave an apologetic smile.

'No. Sorry, no stock.'

'OK. Do you have *Pavarotti in the Park*?'

Another negative response, and an even more apologetic smile.

Four further suggestions followed, each one being met with a sad shake of the head from an increasingly glum assistant.

'Right,' I said, becoming a little impatient. 'I've asked for six different tapes and you haven't had one of them in stock. The notice on your window states, "You ask for it, we have got it". So what's the problem?'

'No problem,' the man replied, a slightly puzzled look spreading across his face at my question. 'We got it. But you not yet asked for it.'

I spent much of today at the Saudi Arabian–Qatari border crossing-point trying to explain to customs officers that seven trucks held there for the past three days with their rear ends pointing towards Saudi and their front ends pointing towards Qatar, and with their documents showing the cargo as manufactured in Saudi and destined for Qatar, and with their drivers in possession of exit visas from Saudi and entry visas into Qatar, and with their cargo marked in large letters 'For Umm Said, Qatar', really did want to cross from Saudi Arabia into Qatar and not in the reverse direction. (Phew. That must be one of the longest opening sentences on record.)

Discussions of this type with customs officers are a regular prelude to establishing the obvious and an exasperating waste of time. They had every intention of eventually allowing the trucks into Qatar but they delight in an argument first. I imagine they do it to improve their English.

Fortunately, as a fatuous barney beats most things for generating an appetite, we resolved the problem with the simple compromise that the trucks leave for Qatar and I buy lunch. The officer and I then adjourned to the local diner conveniently situated nearby.

This was Abdullah's Café, an establishment infamous throughout the region for a menu which offered its patrons one of two choices – take it or leave it. In this joint, if you couldn't smell burning, you knew someone had ordered a salad. On the inside wall, a chewed-up diploma evidenced Abdullah's attendance in 1987 of a cookery course in Dubai sponsored by the local French Embassy. He failed it, of course. Abdullah's culinary abilities are probably best described as just short of homicide.

However, since my previous visit the premises proved to be under the management of a new Abdullah, although there was no evidence of change – nor, indeed, of Abdullah. We sat down at the only table, removing a cat which had been asleep with what remained of its tail wrapped around a ketchup bottle. Interestingly, the cat was blind and the table had only three of its four original legs, two facts which were apparently connected, but I abandoned my attempt at understanding what the hell the customs officer was getting at when he endeavoured to explain the association. The chairs were old upturned packing cases with cushions tied to them and the words 'Property of Qatar Petrochemical Co.' stencilled on the side.

IF THE SUN DOESN'T KILL YOU,

Moments later Abdullah dashed in from the kitchen and wiping his hands on the cat, welcomed us both in his finest English.

'Bye, bye, take a seat, have a cup of tea.'

Nearly everyone out here says this. Take a seat, have a cup of tea. It must be on the first page of the *Teach Yourself English* phrase book on sale in various emporia around Doha. The equivalent to our earliest learnt French phrases like 'The pen of my aunt is dead,' or 'I need urgent medical attention, please direct me to the nearest fishmonger.'

Mine host handed us the menu and a significant improvement immediately became evident as the *à la carte* selection had doubled in size from that on offer under the previous management. There were now two choices of meals. The first option was hot chips/chicken/rice with lettuce salad as the alternative. After appropriate thought, I decided to work through the card.

Abdullah wrote my order meticulously on his sleeve.

'Tea come soon,' he said, and departed with such enthusiasm he stumbled over the cat which had relocated itself on the floor by the kitchen door. Pretending not to notice, the cat held its ground. Having been heaved off the table and used as a towel within the space of five minutes, it wasn't giving up easily. Moments later a smiling Mrs Abdullah appeared clasping two mugs of lemon tea. She also trod on the luckless creature. Obliged by this unprovoked bombardment to adopt emergency action, the cat shot off in a circular movement before curling itself up in precisely the same place. Strange. It was the cat which was blind but everyone else who collided with it.

After five minutes Abdullah returned with an enormous plate on which were heaped both the lettuce salad and the hot chips, chicken and rice. I surveyed my order. The salad seemed fine. Nothing exceptional, but even here there aren't too many surprises to be anticipated from a lettuce salad. The remaining food, however, was satisfactory with regard to only three of its four advertised features. The chips, chicken and rice looked good. But it was in the 'hot' department the meal was conspicuously deficient. In fact, to be blunt, it was stone cold.

I called for Abdullah. He rushed from the kitchen, carefully overstepping the cat before falling over Mrs Abdullah. She was on her hands and knees behind the counter, pursuing a cockroach the size of a tank with an enormous can of spray starch.

'This food cold, Abdullah. Nothing worse than cold, greasy chips. Please make hot.'

Taking back the plate, five minutes later he returned with a cheerful smile and placed the food on the table.

Have you ever tasted hot lettuce?

On my return to the villa late this evening after driving from the border, I found a note shoved through the gate from Kylie and Kurt, inviting me to dinner tomorrow which will be cooked by Kylie. Heavens! In a recent survey, nine out of ten people questioned said they'd rather have a wet night out with Michael Heseltine than eat one of Kylie's dinners.

The note also revealed the evening to be in honour of someone called Barbara who works at the British Embassy in Doha. I wonder what that's all about?

* * * * *

On the occasion of my last meeting with Kylie, I recall concluding she must be the most undernourished-looking woman in Qatar. I was wrong. Barbara is worse. Kylie calls her Barbie, like the doll. And how appropriate.

She reminds me of Olive Oil from the Popeye cartoons. In one episode, whatever she ate became clearly outlined through her vest. If she swallowed a banana whole, there was the shape. Barbie Doll conjures up the same image. If she swallowed a Malteser, so conspicuous would it be, men

127

would offer their seat in the train. Not that we have any trains in Qatar, or indeed many men who would stand up for a woman – pregnant-looking or not. But you get my point.

As I arrived, the two girls were discussing an article from this morning's *Gulf Times* concerning diet. Surely they're not on one? Apparently we only need a daily intake of around 2,500 calories and this particular article illustrated how to reduce this by 10 calories a day without undue effort. But no time limit was mentioned. So what happens after eight months when by my reckoning we'd all be down to a daily intake of no calories whatsoever, I can't imagine. Presumably *The Gulf Times* isn't too concerned about its circulation figures. Incorrect weather forecasts, unreliable horoscopes, barmy stories, questionable features – *The Gulf Times*. Cancel your order today.

Barbie Doll comes from north Wales, singularly appropriate as she'd evidently embarked on a one-woman crusade to sustain its sheep-farming industry. She was knitting when I arrived and apart from a break for dinner devoted the entire evening to creating what I can only imagine must be a second runway for Doha airport. And it's surprising how irritating the click, click, click, click, click, click, click, click, click of needles becomes after the first four hours. The Scarface twins would have fetched them a few hefty clouts had they been around. Working on the switchboard at the British Embassy, her lilting, melodious tones must have beguiled many an eager suitor on the phone, reality only later disgorging the ugly truth. She knits. At twenty-eight years old, the past four of which have been spent in Qatar, she aspires to move on to the United States in a few months. American sheep, watch your backs.

The evening began inauspiciously when Kurt, who appears to become more portly by the day, plonked himself exuberantly next to me on the same end of the settee. It was the subsequent Richter scale 6 earthquake which alerted Kylie to the danger threatening the furniture, one she promptly eliminated by proclaiming Kurt a fat pig and dismissing him into the kitchen to peel onions.

Starting from a low base, Kylie's meal proved less torturous than expected. True, dinner was a lump of grease in the shape of a lamb chop, surrounded by two dozen attendant lumps of grease in the shape of chips. But it was what followed that counted. Doughnuts.

To allow the meal to congeal in comfort, Kurt and I decamped to the lounge where we watched a film on television while the ladies and knitting adjourned into the kitchen to make doughnuts – Barbie Doll's birthday treat. The film was in black and white and called *The Hunter of the Great Kalawongo*. So what can I say about the films on Qatar Television? Nothing really. But here goes anyway.

The English language service of Qatar Television, some of which is indeed in English, transmits from late afternoon until midnight. It consists of a daily diet of old American situation comedies (*I Love Lucy* being a recent acquisition), live Qatari League soccer matches, occasional vintage editions of *Horizon*, and a half-hour news bulletin which rivals even *The Gulf Times* for tedium. There being no equivalent to the *Radio Times*, the pre-planning of essential programmes to avoid can require diligence and a fair sprinkling of good fortune and just because a programme starts, doesn't mean it will necessarily finish.

All transmissions are subject to censorship. Kissing between males and females, or more southerly contact, is not permitted, which prompts a fair amount of reel-jumping as characters about to embrace in the bedroom are instantly despatched downstairs to be seen happily noshing fish fingers and a side salad in the kitchen. And quite right too. Who wants that sort of thing in this heat? Which is where *The Hunter of the Great Kalawongo* came in – as, indeed, did the doughnuts.

Anyone knowing me is aware of my insatiable penchant for doughnuts. Be they round, ring, jam, or cream, just let me at them, and their unavailability in Qatar I've long considered a serious contravention of my civil rights. And to be fair these were a fine effort. No jam or cream, but good nevertheless. Home-producing doughnuts to the standard of commercial bakeries is a task rarely achieved in my experience. Not that the girls were too keen. Despite their exertions, they devoured just one between them.

We watched the film in its entirety. Quite why is unclear, as it proved more incomprehensible than the metric system. Involving a monster moth which simultaneously lived in and ate the Kalawongo jungle, it starred a handsome white hunter and a beautiful heroine, who together slogged off in search of the moth, accompanied by just a native guide, two spears and a spectacular wardrobe of dresses by Dior.

Following a series of bloodcurdling adventures involving man-eating squirrels and a demented toad, the girl was attacked by the moth, but rescued in the nick of time by the hero using the end of his spear. We stuck with the film in the forlorn hope it might eventually respond to patience.

Evil-looking natives in loincloths chucked poisoned darts, before being booted into a raging river to be eaten by what appeared to be a giant haddock. And a worm the length of Chile made short work of the luckless guide. Then the censorial scissors galloped into action and the film ended abruptly, just before the hero and heroine locked into a passionate embrace – the girl in her flawless Revlon make-up looking as glamorous as when she started.

No doubt there are some people who thought *The Hunter of the Great Kalawongo* was a film worth watching. Naturally there will also be others who consider this opinion ridiculous. I agree with the others.

Disregarding the advice of Sybil Fawlty concerning what not to discuss with a German, the four of us then held what transpired to be an earnest debate about war, Kylie proving more sagacious than I'd previously appreciated. She's against all forms of violence, a relief to Kurt, no doubt. And good for her. I played them the eight-minute long, 'And The Band Played Waltzing Matilda' by The Pogues, Eric Bogle's chilling words, of an Australian soldier at the Gallipoli landings during the First World War, graphically illustrating the misery of battle. These things are always subjective, but for me it's the definitive anti-war song.

> And the band played Waltzing Matilda
> As we stopped to bury our slain,
> And we buried ours and the Turks buried theirs,
> Then it started all over again.

Driving Barbie Doll home to her flat, she unexpectedly revealed something which could make the balance of my stay in Qatar inordinately more satisfying. Close to the British Embassy is a shop which sells doughnuts. Fantastic. What would you do if I said I love you, Barbie? I'll be there first thing in the morning.

Back now at the villa, and presumably as a result of gastronomic indiscretion, my sleep has been disturbed by a most unpleasant dream which woke me abruptly just moments ago. It was awful. I was forced into an arranged marriage with Princess Margaret.

✼ ✼ ✼ ✼ ✼

Are you sitting comfortably? Then I'll begin.

Once upon a time there was a jam doughnut. It looked delicious with lots of strawberry jam and masses of snow-white sugar. But sadly, this doughnut had a problem. It was elusive. In fact it was the most elusive jam doughnut the world has ever known. But let me start at the beginning.

The different perspective given to time in Qatar from that which prevails in the more frenetic West, is plainly evidenced by the extraordinary amount of sitting about which goes on. Wherever one looks, in shops, in offices, in garages, in the streets, people are waiting for nothing to happen. It's not that they're unemployed, as everyone has a job in Qatar. But to achieve this admirable objective, an element of overmanning is necessary and is readily accepted into the lifestyle. As a result, time is available in abundance. Which brings us back to the elusive jam doughnut.

Barbie Doll's directions proved faultless. On entering the store my attention was immediately drawn to a lone doughnut sitting forlornly under a perspex cover on the bread counter. Restraining my excitement, I strolled nonchalantly across to the storekeeper.

'Good morning. I'd like to buy that doughnut, please.'

'Of course. Take a seat, have a cup of tea.'

Producing a pair of plastic tongs he began removing the doughnut from its cover, but as he did so it dropped to the floor. Unfortunately, it then bounced back up again, suggesting its condition was less fresh than I'd have wished.

'Oh, dear. Sorry about that.'

'Don't worry,' I replied, disguising my disappointment at this calamitous turn of events. 'I wouldn't have bought it anyway. What time are your doughnuts freshly delivered?'

'Every morning at eight o'clock.'

'OK, I'll be back tomorrow.'

It was a little after eight when I returned. Unusually for Qatar, a blanket of fog had descended during the night. So dense was it first thing, it took practically ten minutes to grope my way through from the bedroom to the kitchen.

Looking along the counter there wasn't a doughnut to be seen.

'Doughnuts?'

The storekeeper looked amazed to even hear the question.

'No. They don't come till eight o'clock.'

'But it's half past eight already.'

'Is it? What day is it?'

'Monday.'

'Monday? Sorry. They don't come on Mondays.'

'Good grief. Will they be here tomorrow?'

'Yes, definitely. Eight o'clock tomorrow morning.'

It was eight o'clock when I returned the next day. Again there was a conspicuous absence of doughnuts. The shopkeeper was waiting, daring me to ask.

'Hello.'

'Hello.'

'Doughnuts?'

'All gone.'

'All gone? But you said eight o'clock and it's now only two minutes past eight. How many did you have?'

'One hundred and fifty.'

'One hundred and fifty and they've all gone?'

'Yes. One woman came in and bought the lot. She was having a party. Did you want some?'

Did I want some! Does a goat smell? Of course I wanted some.

'Right,' I said, taking charge of the situation. 'I'll be back tomorrow. So save me one dozen, please.'

'OK,' he smiled.

At precisely eight o'clock I returned to a counter devoid of anything resembling a doughnut.

'Hello.'

'Hello.'

'Doughnuts?'

'Doughnuts?'

'Where are they?'

'Van not come.'

'Van not come? Please phone your depot and check what time the van's coming.'

'OK. Take a seat, have a cup of tea,' and he disappeared into the rear.

Five minutes later he was back.

'Van broken down.'

'What do you mean van broken down?'

133

'Van broken down, van can't come.'

'How long will it be?'

'Hold on, I'll check.'

Then two minutes later.

'Repair nearly finished. Doughnuts here soon. Please wait. Have a cup of tea.'

'OK,' I said, seeing light at the end of the tunnel, 'I'll wait. What time will the van be here?'

'Half past one.'

'Half past one?' I shrieked. 'But it's only eight o'clock in the morning. You expect me to wait from eight o'clock in the morning until half past one in the afternoon for doughnuts? You must be crazy.'

But he did expect me to wait, which is the serious point of the story. Because time for many people in Qatar is comparatively meaningless. They get up each day to do the limited amount of work available, to earn a limited amount of money, to buy a limited amount of food, and then they go home, go to bed, get up next morning, and they do it all over again.

These people aren't crazy, of course. Just realistic.

12

We regret tonight's performance is cancelled due to incompetence.

Ah, there you are.

Every working day, business documents are despatched to me by courier from London and, because I insisted on it as part of my contract, incorporated with them is a newspaper for that day – normally *The Daily Mail*. I like the *Mail*. It's responsible for my all-time favourite headline.

During the early seventies, the Scottish international forward Gerry Queen was playing in a home FA Cup-tie for Crystal Palace, I think against Leeds. Towards the end of a distinctly boisterous match, there was an almighty dingdong involving most of the players, and then a section of the crowd who invaded the pitch. Once things calmed down, Gerry Queen became one of three players sent off. The following morning the *Daily Mail* headline screamed, 'Queen in punch-up at the Palace'. Good stuff.

Anyway, supplemented by the more circumspect and less reliable transmissions of the BBC World Service – less reliable reception-wise – this daily newspaper gives me a regular insight to events in Britain.

During recent weeks, I've become increasingly depressed by an apparent escalation in violent crime especially against children and girls, and it set me reflecting on the respective merits of the Western and Arab judicial systems. And in particular concerning retribution for crime.

Much has been said on the subject of the draconian punishments enforced by some of the Gulf States for infringement of their laws. This 'You steal and we'll chop your hand off' principle is understandably contentious in the West where public opinion generally rejects such severity – paradoxically while capital punishment still maintains such widespread support. But for what it's worth, mark me down with the Arabs. And for one fundamental reason. Dissuasive punishment works.

I don't wish to preach – which means I'm going to, of course – but look through any edition of *The Gulf Times* and you won't read of children being murdered, women raped, old people mugged, banks robbed, or cars stolen. And why won't you read of such things? Not because the press is censored – which it is – but because they rarely happen. Compared to the West, crime's a bit of a non-event in Qatar. And can you imagine the security that provides? So the system works. And it does so in a country where seventy per cent of the population are non-Arab itinerants, originating from countries with flourishing crime rates. But people here know the rules and for the most part accept them. And why? Because they understand the consequences if they don't.

In recent weeks, British newspapers have reported a seemingly endless series of particularly horrifying crimes, culminating yesterday in news of the murder of a poor girl on Wimbledon Common while her small boy looked on. In the United Kingdom, two people a day are murdered and two crimes of violence committed every minute. A burglary occurs every twenty seconds. And which factors are so frequently blamed for this shocking situation? Alcohol, drugs, sex and violence on television, and inadequate deterrent sentencing of criminals. And what won't you find in Qatar? Alcohol, drugs, sex and violence on television, and inadequate deterrent sentencing of criminals. A coincidence?

It has taken me a year of living in an almost crime-free environment where basic precautions automatically practised in London can be safely disregarded, to recognise the price we all pay in Britain to live in our so-called free democracy. It's idealism, of course, but if only the vociferous freedom-for-the-individual brigade could more readily appreciate the continuing infringement of freedom which crime, not only in its real but also potential form, inevitably inflicts.

Shortly before leaving London last year, I was roped into a charity event which involved being sponsored for three days whilst delivering telephone books to subscribers in East London. My allocated area included the Pembury Estate in Hackney, a collection of five-storey blocks of about 1000 flats built around sixty years ago. There are no lifts.

To pronounce this estate the most deprived in the country would be an exaggeration as regrettably there are many similar examples across Britain. These days official verbosity identifies them as sub-standard inner city housing. I still call them slums. And Pembury was grim. Every member of the government – any government – should be obliged to live for a week in a place like this to witness the circumstances in which some of the society they represent must live. Old people – no, most people – with doors and windows barricaded, frightened to venture from their homes even during the day. Graffiti everywhere – foul-languaged incitement against the police, the government, ethnic groups and much of society. It's no wonder children raised in conditions such as these have no regard for authority and crime becomes instinctive. How incongruous a single window-box seemed, boldly revealing a glimpse of colour in this profusion of brick, concrete and gloom. And one incident exemplified the despair.

As I stood in the courtyard preparing to ascend the stairs for the umpteenth time whilst laden with books, a woman approached the stairway pushing a pram containing two young children. She also had two large bags of shopping hanging from the handles. Reaching the foot of the stairs she smiled wryly in my direction.

'It's the usual choice. Either I carry the kids up and the shopping will probably be gone when I get back, or I grab the shopping and risk the kids being taken.'

Undoubtedly there's accommodation in Qatar, the Paradise Estate in Umm Said for one, which is residentially inferior to Pembury. But the occupants don't have the crime to contend with. They don't live in fear.

So you'll not persuade me the occasional loss of a hand, or indeed a head, isn't warranted by the benefits of living free from the constant anxiety of attack, not only on yourself, but also your family and property. True, I may be indulging in oversimplification of a complex subject. But having now experienced life under two distinct judicial philosophies, I know which leaves me feeling most secure. Arabs believe the emphasis should be on resolute protection of the majority. And they believe this is justified. And the more I consider it, the greater merit there seems in the system here. And if it does contain injustice, then only the lawbreakers suffer. The rest of us just have the damn great holes in the roads to worry about.

Incidentally, although limited consolation for the recipient, on the rare occasions a hand is amputated, the law requires the thief to be anaesthetised before amputation and subsequently treated in hospital. Also the State becomes responsible for his welfare for the remainder of his life.

✻ ✻ ✻ ✻ ✻

Today is National Traffic Day in Qatar and we drivers have all been confronted with a most unexpected development.

THE WASHING MACHINE WILL

The front page of *The Gulf Times* has this morning revealed the official speed limits which apply for driving here, the first occasion any of us have seen them in print – or indeed were aware they existed.

For private cars the limit is 60 kilometres an hour in Doha and 100 kilometres outside. Allowing for the latest underlying trends, this equates to 37 and 62 miles an hour. For commercial vehicles the limit in Doha corresponds to just 25 miles an hour. We weren't advised the method by which the authorities arrived at these figures, but suspect it may be connected with the influence of the European Fixed Exchange Rate Mechanism on the Qatari riyal – either that or it's as fast as the police cars will go.

To further make the point, *The Gulf Times* also advises that the authorities intend to enforce these speed limits using mobile radar gun devices made in Britain. Unfortunately these aren't due to arrive in Qatar for approximately six months. Maybe they're being delivered by trucks observing the new 25-mile-an-hour restriction.

In addition to the radar, a number of strategically placed billboards will be erected on the main highways which will apparently state 'Drive Slow – Less Accidnets' (sic). Indeed!

To date, a careful driver in Qatar has been conspicuously evident as the one with all four of his vehicle's wheels in contact with the road, pavement, or someone else's front garden at approximately one and the same time. But no longer.

So what changes can we expect from this forthcoming eruption of more leisurely and responsible driving? No more will we hear the familiar twice-daily sonic boom as the Bangladeshi school bus builds up speed on the Umm Said–Doha highway, carrying its horde of singing infants. No longer will passengers in aircraft en route to Doha Airport, look down in fascination as they're undertaken by ninety per cent of the vehicles below. No longer will pedestrians need a packed lunch when attempting to cross the Doha ring road. But back to *The Gulf Times*.

We are also informed a Traffic City will be constructed 'bristling with numerous fun facilities to inculcate [*huh?*] safety awareness amongst Qatar's drivers. This will be built adjacent to the zoo.' The zoo? Give that man a medal. What a masterstroke of perceptive planning. But we're not finished yet.

'To celebrate National Traffic Day, the Traffic Department yesterday evening hosted a dinner for Qatar's best drivers who had driven for more than thirty years without accidents.' It omitted to specify how many drivers were invited, but there were only two bicycles parked outside when I passed the Traffic Department last night.

The article concluded with a message from the Director of Traffic who disclosed a substantial number of road accidents – sorry, accidnets – were caused by drivers wearing sandals which became stuck between the brake and the accelerator, and he proposed henceforth the wearing of sandals should be avoided whilst driving. That's a puzzle as the occasions on which drivers in Qatar place their feet even remotely within sticking distance of the brake are few indeed.

While returning from Umm Said to Doha this evening, I noticed the first of the billboards being erected alongside the highway. And sure enough it advised in enormous letters, and with commendable perception, 'Drive Slow – Less Accidnets'. Quite right. And Paint Slow – Less Mistakes.

To conclude, it would seem a wasted opportunity not to express my own confidence in the success of these reforms. But what's one more wasted opportunity? There'll be tears before the jelly I'll be bound.

I'm back again concerning the new speed limits. Without wishing to sound like Esther Rantzen, conscience demands my acknowledgement of the merit in these latest measures. This country sits uneasily with radical innovation – like those the world over. I remember the time pot noodles first hit the shops in Britain. But road safety is a serious business and any attempts by the Qatari authorities to reduce accidents are welcome and to be applauded. Right. Now I can go to sleep.

* * * * *

The deeply upsetting news came to me yesterday that Vincent is in jail. The circumstances are difficult to establish. His friends understand he's been sentenced to two years following investigations by the police concerning visa irregularities. I've no grounds for questioning his conviction. Although no jury system exists, merely a bench of independent judges, Qatar isn't a country where individuals are thrown into jail without perceived justification.

But whatever the true circumstances, the implications for Vincent and his family are serious. His wife and children must return to their homeland as soon as arrangements can be made, their residency being allied to Vincent's work permit which is automatically revoked. Vincent himself will be deported at the completion of his sentence. Who now assists his wife and kids and pays their return flights remains to be seen. Hopefully his community friends will support them. The disgrace brought on the family is less easily handled.

I made a series of telephone calls to establish the visiting regulations at the jail which appeared to vary in accordance with the duty roster. Once substantiated, I drove there this evening with a box of food and drink. It's incumbent on relatives and friends of a prisoner to bring appropriate sustenance, otherwise the diet provided by the authorities is limited to the minimum necessary to sustain health.

On arrival I was asked to meet the duty captain who explained that whilst I was permitted to see Vincent, his personal recommendation was that I didn't. As he'd previously worked for me, the captain considered Vincent would feel so demeaned at my knowledge of his situation, any succour gained from the visit would be more than negated. Accepting this logic, I changed plans and deposited the provisions with the captain. He agreed to deliver them on the pretext they were donated by friends.

Meanwhile, I can only hope his undoubted resilience and belief in God support him in what's certain to be a protracted ordeal. Good luck, Vincent.

✳ ✳ ✳ ✳ ✳

It's not often you can earn money for staring at a brown and mauve striped curtain for fifty minutes. But I did last week. And the pay-off came today.

The office in Umm Said which co-ordinates the North Field Project, employs immigrants from many countries including the Philippines, whose nationals have two renowned characteristics. First, in relation to the average Westerner, they're short. A British chin is as far as the majority will ever get. Second, they're notoriously industrious in even the most adverse conditions – which is why a substantial community exists in Qatar.

In recent months, I've had contact with one in particular of these workers from the Philippines whose name – wait for it – is Philip. Or that's what everyone calls him. Towards the end of last year he introduced me to the music of Kitaro, a Japanese keyboard player of whom I'd not previously heard. Kitaro is a superstar in the Far East and Philip lent me several of his albums which I've copied on to tapes. These now regularly accompany me in the car as the stirring music is made for desert driving.

Last week, discovering Philip to be less enthusiastic in the office than normal, I enquired as to the cause. He'd only recently returned following four days in hospital for repairs to his face which was severely blistered when he neglected to stand back after opening his car door one lunch-time.

And a right mess he looked. The accumulation of heat inside a car standing in the midday summer sun is all but indescribable. If you don't wait several seconds after opening the door before attempting to enter, the old saying 'It's like having hot soup thrown in your face' is as accurate as you're likely to get. Whenever possible, windows are left partially unwound to avoid the problem, but blowing sand often makes this impracticable. So we all remember not to dive straight into our cars. Or most of us do.

However it was not this misfortune which caused Philip's dejection, but an impending visit to Doha by a female singer from the Philippines, a major star in her country. She was to perform a single concert for the Filipino community here. Such was the demand for tickets that both the geographical disadvantage of living in Umm Said, and the ticket cost, given his meagre earnings, had precluded him from obtaining any before the show sold out. What a pity. But aside from offering him a couple of my favourite Elizabeth Shaw Mint Crisp Chocolates, a box of which is sent to me weekly from London (that's also in my contract), there was little to be done to console the lad for his disappointment.

The following evening while listening to Tim's radio programme during the drive back to Doha, my attention was drawn to a station bulletin. Incidentally, it has little relevance to this specific episode, none whatsoever in fact, but I've observed a conspicuous tarting-up of Qatar Radio recently. Gone are the unfathomable announcers with their five-minute programmes and ten-minute silences. Their replacements are of an altogether more proficient standard. Well done someone. My only reservation concerns a delectable sounding Scottish girl who's just appeared. She must be related to the guy working in the Weather Department as I can't understand a word she says. It must be me. Mr Al-Khalifi was at the villa last night and even he grasped what the girl was on about. Did I mention he has an Australian wife?

So I was driving home in the car when my attention was drawn to this station bulletin. As yet another Stevie Ray Vaughan track faded away Tim, using his special official announcements voice, revealed this enticing information.

'After that great Stevie Ray Vaughan track,' – oh, yeh, says who, Tim? – 'Qatar Radio is proud to advise we are in possession of two tickets for the Filipino concert tomorrow night in Doha. All others have been sold, so this is now your only opportunity to see the performance. The next track on the turntable is 'One More Night' by Phil Collins and the first person to call the studio on 894422 and give me the name of the group Phil Collins leads will win the tickets.'

That's too easy, Tim, I thought. You've let yourself in for trouble there. Your lines will be jammed for hours.

Frankly, choosing a musical subject is a departure for Qatar Radio competitions as the format normally applied is to set a question relating to a more cultural, environmental, or Arabic issue. Something akin to how many legs on a camel?

Curious to know whether the response to this contest had indeed been overwhelming, having arrived back at the villa and extracted one of the chickens from inside an upturned aluminium bucket, I phoned the studio. I had only a limited expectation of getting through, despite it being more than an hour since the announcement of the contest. But the line connected and was answered by Tim.

'Hi, I thought you'd be engaged. I bet you've been inundated about this competition. It's your own fault. Why didn't you make it more difficult?'

'No, yours is the first call. Drop round this evening after the show and you can collect the tickets.'

'But I haven't given you the answer.'

'Don't worry about that. I can't remember the question anyway. And someone's got to have them. Incidentally, what was the answer? I'd better announce it over the air.'

'The Rolling Stones. 'Bye.'

How strange. Evidently not a single Filipino in Qatar knew who the hell Phil Collins was, and no Westerners, who would have known, harboured the slightest interest in wasting two hours of good sleeping time watching an unknown foreigner chirruping away. So I had two tickets for the show. What a turn up.

The following day I informed Philip of my good fortune and flamboyantly presented him with the tickets. To see his excitement and gratitude was worth all the effort I hadn't made in obtaining them. But life has a cruel way of rewarding the virtuous. Philip, not appreciating the implications of what he was saying, insisted I accompany him. It proved impossible to refuse. Oh, for the merciful release of death.

And so it was, that less than a year after the Albanian Dance and Accordion Group fiasco at which time I vowed never to set foot in the place again, five days ago I found myself attending a cultural evening in the same theatre and awaiting the appearance of this Filipina singer. And awaiting the appearance of this Filipina singer. And awaiting the appearance of this Filipina singer. And awaiting . . .

Due to a fracas between Scarface 1 and the chickens which my dexterity swiftly resolved, I arrived at the theatre a little after the advertised starting time. I'm becoming so expert these days, David Attenborough phones me. The place was packed with about three hundred Filipinos, all sitting in silence and looking at a brown and mauve striped curtain still drawn across the stage. I joined Philip and for fifty minutes awaited some indication we hadn't congregated a day early.

Then without warning a diminutive man wearing a crumpled, black satin suit dashed on. This was the theatre manager. On closer inspection, even by Filipino standards, diminutive may have been an over-generous description.

'If it ever rains again in Qatar,' Philip whispered, 'this man will be last to know.'

Giving a sickly grin, he lunged in the direction of the microphone to announce the show was cancelled as the singer had missed her flight from the Philippines. I'm sorry? Could you repeat that? Giving a sickly grin he lunged in the direction of the microphone to announce the show was cancelled as the singer had missed her flight from the Philippines. But surely as the flying time from Manila to Qatar is about eight hours, it's inconceivable this man wasn't aware long before we all assembled that the show couldn't possibly commence? Yet not only did no one bother to advise the cancellation, but we were then kept waiting for practically an hour before being informed by way of this asinine excuse.

Philip had obviously taken a dislike to him.

'What's the difference between the theatre manager and a bucket of camel dung?' he asked.

I raised an enquiring eyebrow.

'The bucket.'

However, the most productive part of the evening was still to come as this nitwit instructed us all to leave in an orderly manner and collect refunds from the office outside. So I received 120 riyals for two tickets I hadn't bought in the first place, just for staring at a brown and mauve striped curtain. Life can be very rewarding on occasions. Philip was less perturbed about the affair than I expected. His cut from the ticket proceeds doubtless helped.

The performance was subsequently rearranged for last night, and Philip told me this afternoon there were just eleven people in the audience. That's one of the things I like about Filipinos. They have an excellent sense of justice. Amongst the absentees was the theatre manager who, according to a notice displayed at the entrance, was in hospital for a minor operation. On his brain no doubt.

✳ ✳ ✳ ✳ ✳

THE WASHING MACHINE WILL

A university in the United States, presumably with nothing better to do, has released details of a survey conducted into tea drinking around the world. This includes a league table based on average consumption during 1991. And it makes riveting reading.

The top three tea-consuming countries on a per capita basis in reverse order, are as follows. And a moment while I open the envelope.

In third place. India. No surprise there.

In second place. The United Kingdom. One lower than I'd have expected.

And in first place, the world's highest consumer of tea per person is . . . Qatar.

It's all here in *The Gulf Times*. My MD in London advised me on the phone today this information was printed last week in *The Daily Express*, so it's obviously true. It must be down to that English phrase book everyone buys. Although on reflection, maybe the news isn't that breathtaking given the limited selection of beverages available here.

Nevertheless, 11 September 1992 marks another memorable date in the history of Qatar. I foresee dancing in the streets tonight. And perhaps a commemorative stamp.

Personally, I can't stand the stuff.

＊ ＊ ＊ ＊ ＊

What you are about to read is a true story. A true story of the unexpected. All the characters are real people. Only the bad language has been changed to protect the sensitive.

Dealing with individuals at the Road Works Department in Doha can be an interminable business, as, like the check-out desks at my local Asda in London, very few are operating at the same time. Yes, I have had problems with my local branch of Asda. On the occasion of my last visit, one of their own staff asked me if I knew the location of the tinned button mushrooms. I do apologise. Back to the matter in hand.

If you eventually succeed in unearthing someone in the

Department prepared to show at least some pretence of interest, as likely as not you'll find yourself up against a brick wall. (That's another well-worn cliché. So much for a grammar school education.)

My villa is the first, or last, of five such residences in a small cul-de-sac, the surface of which is compacted sand and rock. On several mornings recently, I've been awoken at five o'clock by the sound of road drills and rock-breakers preparing trenches prior to the installation of sewage pipes. Despite this being thirty minutes earlier than my usual waking time, a disturbance of this sort is not as unreasonable as first seems, much of Qatar being a hive of activity before six o'clock when many of the offices and shops begin their day.

Emerging from the villa yesterday before leaving for work, I observed that the various trenches dug during recent days were now linked to form an excavation about eight feet long, six feet deep and the full width of the road. Before driving off using the far end of the cul-de-sac, I spoke with the three workers in an attempt to establish the duration of their assignment as even the loss of half an hour's sleep can accumulate into something more than inconvenience.

Our conversation was not significantly productive, inevitably so when four individuals are blathering on in four different languages, with the waving of arms constituting the prime means of effective communication. And what was all that mysterious pointing at the sky? Surely not weather permitting? It's eleven months since we last had rain.

Eventually I understood the pipe was to be laid and the trench re-filled that same day, and the following morning the digging of one last trench would commence with, I was categorically assured, minimal disruption to residents. But that, as Paul McCartney may have said, was yesterday.

At precisely five o'clock this morning the bedlam began, although sounding more distant than of late. As the kitchen clock had fallen off the wall and almost disembowelled

Scarface 2, who then required a lengthy period of consoling and reassurance before he felt ready to face the world, it was almost seven o'clock before I left the villa and entered the car for the journey to work.

Immediately I perceived a new trench had indeed appeared, of approximately similar proportions to yesterday's, but on this occasion dug across the other end of the cul-de-sac. In itself, this would have been quite acceptable had they not omitted to refill their effort of the previous day. So in a nutshell, and not to over-dramatise the situation, I was trapped.

Five minutes of arm waving with the workmen failed to extract any indication that they appreciated the significance of their well-intentioned action.

'No problem,' said one, two words which inevitably hide a significant complication. The wise give up here.

'Finish soon. Pleese you wait.'

'When finish?'

A forlorn shrug of the shoulders constituted his only response. We could be talking in days.

With little alternative but to walk to the nearest main road, I then took a taxi to my office before later confronting the brains of the Road Works Department. It was a waste of time, of course. And if I hear the words 'no problem' again!!!

I spoke with the man in charge of trenches in the road, as well as the man in charge of the man in charge of trenches in the road. From what I could deduce, each of them was aware of one of the trenches, but not of the other. And it was quite evident neither had a clue what their colleague had organised in the past, or had planned for the future. How can a country which builds such magnificent mosques be responsible for this? And those insipid explanations. I don't know which was more irritating. The fact number one trench man had no idea what his deputy was up to, or the weak excuses dished out by number two. Talk about the blind leading the bland.

What would Qatar be without men like those at the Road Works Department? Frankly, I'd be quite prepared to find out.

Not that Qatar is the only current example of corporate ambivalence. BBC World Service has just advised of extraordinary goings-on in London yesterday, apparently dubbed Black Wednesday. It seems interest rates increased and decreased about fifteen times in the space of twenty minutes. Why Black Wednesday I can't imagine, as given Britain's prevailing massive financial deficit, Red Wednesday would seem more fitting.

Had I been a British taxpayer, which currently I'm not, I'd have a few words to say about the way the country's presently being governed – in particular with respect to competence. But I'm not. So I won't.

And whilst on the subject of the right hand not knowing etc., Moira enlightened me recently that in the same way humans are normally either predominantly left- or right-handed, cats also share this characteristic. That's interesting, isn't it?

I tested this theory on the Scarface twins, undertaking an exhaustive research programme which basically involved bouncing a table-tennis ball at them for fifteen minutes and recording which paw they clouted it with. And Moira's information was spot-on. In this independent survey, two out of two cats tested chose the left paw. And being left-handed myself that seemed eminently appropriate.

Scarface 1 was 100 per cent on every occasion. But 2 was slightly less convincing, his deficiency in the left eye department perhaps accounting for his paw performance. I wonder if other animals have this left or right bias? I'd check the goats but they might get the impression I'm interested in them.

I've been looking forward to relating this information to you all day. Which shows what an exciting life I lead.

*

One of my car windscreen wipers disappeared two nights ago while the vehicle was outside the villa. An eyewitness report indicated the suspect to be a black male, approximately three feet tall, with a beard and malodorous aura. Enough said. No need for an identikit picture to guess it was one of the goats.

As the local motor agent is located about fifteen miles from Doha, to avoid a wasted journey I first telephoned to establish whether a replacement wiper was in stock. Receiving confirmation, I drove to the garage.

After waiting for thirty minutes in a queue comprising myself, an assistant leapt eagerly into view. I requested the wiper, and following a spirited inspection of the spares catalogue,

'Sorry. Problem. No stock.'

'No stock? But I telephoned only an hour ago and you told me you had one.'

'Sorry. Now sold.'

'So when did you sell it?'

'Hold on, I check. Yes. Sold six months ago.'

I relate this episode to explain, or excuse more likely, my disgraceful behaviour this morning when my telephone line became crossed with that of a local garage. It's no justification, but retribution does on occasions make one feel extraordinarily content.

My phone first rang at about seven o'clock. A man wanted his car serviced.

'How long will it take?'

'Three months.'

'Three months?' he repeated sounding astonished.

'Oh, sorry. We're a bit busy at the moment. It's four months.'

The line went dead. Then ten minutes later we were off again.

'It's Mrs Green here. I'm ringing from the British Embassy about my car you repaired yesterday. When it was returned,

151

the front seat was covered in grease and there were cigar-ette burns on the steering wheel.'

'Oh dear,' I said, 'are you sure you didn't request our special seat greasing and wheel burning service?'

'I certainly did not. I shall write and complain.' And she hung up.

About an hour later – ring ring.

'I want to speak to the Manager,' a man shouted rudely. He sounded the sort who'd leave banana skins outside an old-people's home.

'Speaking.'

'This is Svensson, the Manager of the Sands Hotel. For the last time where is my BMW?'

'Your BMW, sir? Let me see. Ah, yes, I'm using it.'

The man's voice soared two octaves. 'You're what?' he shrieked.

'I'm using it,' I repeated. 'We like to drive all our cus-tomers' cars, sir. It's to ensure they've been correctly repaired and because it saves us from buying our own.'

'This is disgraceful,' screamed Svensson, a pair of tonsils lodging themselves firmly in my ear. 'I want my car back immediately otherwise I'll contact the police.'

'Oh dear. Could it possibly wait until after the weekend? I'm entered in the Dubai Desert Rally and your car would be ideal.'

The man bawled a tirade of abuse, and then the line went dead.

Ten minutes later we were on the move again.

'Mr Abdoun here. I left my van with you yesterday. Have you changed the oil?'

'Ah, yes, I remember. It was so old, we kept the oil and changed the van.'

Soon after lunch the fault on my line was corrected by the engineers. Which was a pity as I'd not had more fun in a month of Fridays. Of course, memory playing the tricks it does, this may not be a verbatim transcript of my conversations. But it's as close as matters.

And now for the weather forecast and sport.

✳ ✳ ✳ ✳ ✳

The pro/anti British monarchy debate was never one to monopolise an excessive measure of my time, although by nature I lean towards the pro camp. However, seen from afar, the current bugged tapes and holiday photographs shenanigans involving Mr and Mrs Heir to the Throne and Mr and Mrs Fourth in Line, seem inappropriate in the extreme, even to the point of impairing the whole concept of a monarchal system.

Candidly, I find it all somewhat disappointing. There have long been many who subscribe to the view that royalty should emerge from its cloistered existence and join the rest of us in the real world. And now some of them have. Personally, I blame far too much sex and violence on television.

✳ ✳ ✳ ✳ ✳

I was horrified to hear on the BBC World Service today that the Queen Mother has been arrested for vandalising a phone box in Basildon. At least I think that's what they said. Maybe not. It's about time someone in London acted to improve reception quality. The programmes frequently give every indication of being transmitted from inside a camel's hump. Doubtless they sound entirely adequate at their end, but they should hear how they emerge in Qatar.

Numerous experiments with my Sony short-wave have demonstrated the only sure technique for obtaining anything that approaches reasonable reception is to position myself on the kitchen table, with the radio in one hand and a 6-foot-long metal pole pointing towards London in the other. The cats think I'm potty.

Being the sort you could take home to your mother, it's

153

my usual practice to remove both boots prior to clambering on the table. Last Saturday whilst I listened to the football results, Scarface 2 did its business in one of them before falling asleep on the other. And once again I missed the majority of the scores, the sound vanishing entirely halfway through the Spurs result. It reached 'Tottenham Hotspurs nil, Manchester City . . .' then nothing. But I knew Spurs had lost. It was the inflection in the reader's voice. It never fails. Home, away, draw. You can always tell before he's finished. One day that regular bloke will retire and we'll all be sunk.

I've just concluded a letter of complaint to the BBC at Bush House in London. After completing the first paragraph which partially outlined my reception difficulties, I reduced the size of my writing until it faded out altogether. Then having left two lines blank, I resumed the correspondence in minute letters which gradually reverted to normal. Two paragraphs on, I repeated the exercise. Perhaps that will adequately illustrate the problem. As a p.s. I requested they serialise on their *Book at Bedtime* programme the new Sue Lawley autobiography which was recently reviewed on the World Service. As best I could gather it's called *My Life As A Bangkok Sex Nymph*.

13
It was the washing machine what dun it.

I was born in London, I've lived most of my life in London, and anyone who doesn't know me can be assured my voice accurately reflects this background – more Michael Caine than Laurence Olivier. And why am I telling you this? Because half an hour ago I became enmeshed in a rather strange conversation with the British Council in Doha.

Starting next Saturday, it's British Commercial Festival Week in Qatar and on my desk is the official programme of events. This includes an English essay competition with two tickets to watch a performance by a visiting Mauritanian folk-dance troupe as first prize. I wonder if second prize is four t . . . ? No, forget it. I'm not dragging that one out.

Despite not writing an essay since leaving school, I decided to enter this competition to show support for the Festival and so phoned the British Council. My call was answered by a woman with a dulcet Welsh voice. Her name was Gaynor. And yes she did know Barbie Doll. And no she wasn't as grotesquely thin. I didn't really ask her that.

After a brief chat, Gaynor transferred me to a woman on the enquiry desk.

'Good morning, I'd like to enter the essay competition.'

'Excellent, we welcome as much support as possible. Can I take a few details?'

For the next ten minutes she demanded a welter of pointless information. All the usual piffle. What is your name? What is your height? Do you play a saxophone in your room after ten o'clock at night? Is there too much snooker on television? Are you prepared to submit to an AIDS test? Am I the most nosey tart the British Council has ever employed? The questions seemed endless. Then just as I was anticipating being asked who won the World Cup in 1966, the woman said,

'OK, that's almost all. Finally, what is your natural tongue?'

'Excuse me,' I replied, 'I don't quite understand.'

'Which language were you brought up with and do you normally speak at home?'

'English,' I said, somewhat taken aback. And with good cause. This was tantamount to talking with the Queen for ten minutes and then asking if she was Bolivian.

'Oh, sorry. The competition's not open to natural speakers of the English language.'

So the English essay competition organised by the British Council for the British Commercial Festival Week, isn't open to Brits. Which is maybe for the best as imagine how embarrassing it would have been to be placed tenth behind five Arabs, three Italians and a Thai. So I gallantly withdrew my application to give a chance to non-natural speakers of the English language.

I understand from nosey tart that the British Council will soon be organising a Tchaikovsky piano competition which will be open to everyone. She wasn't too certain of the precise details but it wouldn't surprise me if we had to guess the weight of the piano.

I've just noticed the official programme of events for this British Commercial Festival Week, includes a gardening competition with categories for flowers and vegetables. The latter interests me as I attempted some basic agriculture when first arriving here, after discovering the cost of a lettuce in Qatar is only marginally less than a two-week holiday in the Virgin Islands.

My London office posted me a packet of lettuce seeds and I obtained a bag of earth from the garden of the Pakistani Embassy. (They'll sell you anything.) Having evicted the duck from an old tin bath in the courtyard, I filled the container with the earth before planting both the seeds and a few onion bulbs. Advising the livestock to keep their distance as it was nothing to do with them, I watered the bath which I then placed at the rear of the villa to derive maximum benefit from the heat and humidity of a Qatari summer. Sadly, like cat flaps, this proved better in theory than it did in practice.

Three days later the onions were the size of Sellafield and I needed a 15-foot extension ladder to reach the top of the lettuces. It's the last time I try agriculture in the summer. I attempted to eat a lettuce but found it so tough, the bath it grew in would have been more palatable. And even the goats declined to tackle the onions. Mr Al-Khalifi suggested I should have put fertiliser on the lettuces. I said I preferred salad cream. He thought that hugely funny. I can't imagine why.

But as it's cooler now, and some of the seeds still remain in the packet, I'll definitely enter the vegetable growing competition. I wonder if nosey tart will require the nationality of the lettuce?

* * * * *

I've been watching the United States presidential election for most of the night relayed from CNN Television, and Clinton has made it. A Democrat in the White House after so many years of Republicanism. Based on just a few newsclips from Qatar Television, he seems a flamboyant, although cosmetic character. One thing is certain. His type would never be elected in the United Kingdom. Far too flash. Mrs Thatcher apart, we prefer our leaders to be dreary. But good luck to him. At least he looks like he'd stay awake during a crisis.

It's the style and panache of an American presidential election which creates such an appealing extravaganza. And so contrasting to a general election in the U.K. Nothing highlights more graphically the distinction between the British and the Americans than their respective elections. A number of Texans work on the North Field Project at Umm Said and, for the most part, treat life much as though it was one continuing presidential campaign. Conversely the British perception appears more allied to the aftermath of an election. Heads down. Only five more years to go.

✳ ✳ ✳ ✳ ✳

Call me a venerable sceptic, or indeed a silly old scoffer, but I've yet to embrace the vagaries of superstition and find myself frequently astonished by those who allow their normal routine to be affected by such arrant claptrap. Take Moira and Kylie. They live by horoscopes. Yet the two most distressing events of my life have occurred on a Friday the 13th in past years, and yesterday I suffered quite my worst experience in Qatar. And today is Saturday the 14th.

Undoubtedly the fact three significant misfortunes have now conspired to hit me on this date of disrepute – which I make odds of 1,380,514 to 1 – represents an intriguing phenomenon which is beyond me to explain. But the role played by the Desert Rose in precipitating yesterday's unfortunate turn of events, I can describe.

The desert is not the compelling, romantic place some quixotics would have us believe and in reality is usually unremittingly tedious. Nevertheless, it occasionally reveals covert wonders and one such is the Desert Rose. This sand-coloured, coral-like substance is confined to sporadic tracts in a few of the world's deserts, notably in Algeria and Saudi Arabia, as before it can form it requires the presence of two uncommon constituents in the sand, gypsum and an underground salt water source. Over the generations this combination produces crystals which develop into a solid mass and a shape reminiscent of a rose petal – hence the name. Concentrate. I'll be asking questions later. In time, each petal creates more petals which form at varying angles, frequently producing remarkable configurations. Due to their scarcity, the exportation of Desert Roses is forbidden – and no one should argue with that.

It was my landlord who acquainted me with this information and also revealed the existence of a small area near the Qatari–Saudi border where they're located. His scepticism regarding my ability to find them was a provocation impossible to ignore.

And so it was that having arranged to telephone Mr Al-Khalifi an hour after sunset to confirm my safe return, a wise precaution when travelling into the desert, I embarked on a journey of exploration with no concern for the date. I was equipped with ten pints of water, a compass, a map from my landlord and a cassette of Mahler's Second Symphony, emotively appropriate for the occasion. It had been Kurt's intention to join me, but he phoned shortly before departure to say that Kylie had demanded his presence indoors to complete a selection of jobs around the house. Black leading the grate or something equally ridiculous, no doubt.

The drive southwards through the desert was predictably uneventful, the tedium broken only by a brief sighting of a group of the bizarre white camels occasionally found in this part of Arabia, and then by a quartet of the black species which were wandering across the road. As I stopped to give them precedence, they did likewise and stood inertly straddled before me. Seven thousand square miles of desert and we had a dispute over right of way. They seemed impressed with Mahler. It's curious how certain music assumes a new distinction in the context of the desert. The Mahler, magnificent at any time, becomes positively ethereal. Verdi has the same quality. And Chas and Dave.

The map Mr Al-Khalifi supplied proved of less assistance than anticipated as it featured Bahrain city centre. Nevertheless, more by providence than enlightened navigation, by recalling his verbal directions of yesterday, within an hour I'd reached and identified the place where it was necessary to divert from the road on to a desert track. A further fifteen minutes driving at precisely twenty miles an hour as instructed then brought me to the point at which wheels had to be abandoned due to increasingly mobile sand.

The concluding section of the journey involved a thirty-minute walk in a south-westerly direction, which Mr Al-Khalifi had assured would bring me to the approximate location of the Desert Roses.

'From then on Mr Peter, it's up to you.'

For about an hour I searched in an apparently futile quest. No wonder so few people have seen the damn things. Then suddenly there they were, in three separate clusters each about the size of a football pitch. There were thousands of them, ranging in diameter from a few inches to about 2 feet, the beauty of their amazing shapes enhanced by the desolate setting in which they lay, its complete absence of sound crudely violated by the crunch of my boots through the sand. And perhaps the most remarkable aspect was their autonomy. Unlike pieces of fragmented rock, each Desert Rose had formed individually from the next. They could have been plucked from the sand like lettuces from a garden.

For nearly an hour I remained enthralled, contemplating this phenomenon constructed from grains of sand into solid, petal-like formations which had multiplied and fashioned themselves into eccentric shapes, some of which depicted animals and birds in such specific detail it was difficult to believe they'd not been artificially created. It was disconcerting to recall a real world existed only a few hours away.

Two hours before sunset, I left the Desert Roses to their seclusion and began the long walk back to the car. And to cut a short story even shorter, the car wouldn't start. Great!

Being to motor mechanics what Neil Kinnock is to winning elections, I soon exhausted all methods I knew of starting a vehicle – namely turning the ignition key to the right. That left plan B. However as this amounted to shrieking 'What the bloody hell can I do now?' at the top of my voice, it proved dismally unproductive. Something more positive was required.

Right, I thought. I've got ninety minutes of daylight remaining and a trek of about forty-five minutes along the track to the road for a possible lift back to Doha.

I was aware that failure to reach the road within the forty-five minutes, and with half the remaining daylight time spent, would compel my return to the car irrespective of how close I might be. In the desert, if there's a new moon, darkness means precisely that. And night is when the desert vipers emerge, and anyone standing on one of those would be lucky to witness another Friday the 13th. Or even another day.

There are two things it's best not to stand on in Qatar – three if you count Kylie – desert vipers, and stone fish which lie along the shore. They resemble stones and inject poison into the foot, which gives the unfortunate recipient a maximum of thirty minutes to find expert treatment, before paralysis and death. So if you fancy a swim, keep your boots on. And look out for the poisonous eels, sharks, sea snakes and giant noxious jellyfish.

Forty-five minutes elapsed with no sign of my objective and the dunes obscuring any indication of its proximity. With great reluctance I began the trudge back to the cause of my misfortune.

161

IF THE SUN DOESN'T KILL YOU,

For some inexplicable reason darkness arrived five minutes early yesterday and before I'd reached the car, visibility
had ebbed away. With increasing apprehension I kept on
walking. Am I still advancing in a straight line, I thought? Or
am I already drifting in a circle on the verge of delirium? And
what if I meet a camel? God, I hope it's a white one. I'll have
no chance distinguishing a black.

You should see the bruise on my kneecap where I walked
into the car. But at least I found it. Folding myself inside, I
wondered how long it would take Mr Al-Khalifi to realise
that the absence of a telephone call confirming my safe
return to Doha indicated a need for assistance. It would take
him three hours to get here I concluded, and awaited my
rescue.

Considering its tranquillity by day, the desert is an alarm-
ingly restless place at night. Heaven knows what all the
noise was about. But I preferred not to know.

Mr Al-Khalifi failed to materialise, presumably unable to
locate my position, and I spent a night of utter tedium
enclosed in a capsule of impenetrable darkness. Other than
being dead or at a country and western festival, nothing
could have been worse. How do internees cope for infinite
periods with only their minds for company? Terry Waite and
the like have my uncomprehending admiration.

Eventually I fell asleep a few minutes before my watch
alarm woke me for the dawn slog back down the track to the
road and transport to Doha.

Once at the roadside it was an hour before I heard the
sound of a vehicle approaching. Due to dawn mist rolling in
from the sea, precise identification was impossible, but the
engine sounded powerful – a BMW perhaps, or a Volvo. Just
the luxury I needed after an uncomfortable night in the car.
Out from the swirl emerged an open truck with eight live
goats in the back. Just great. Symbolism at a time like
this.

Responding to my lukewarm wave, the driver brought his

vehicle to an unnecessarily abrupt halt, sending the goats into a confused tumbling heap. After my night in the desert, I exuded a fragrance comparable to all eight and wondered if he might insist I join them in the back. As he lowered the window and muttered God knows what to me in Arabic, I noticed he bore an uncanny resemblance to his load. He spoke no English and his leathered, sun-creased face gave him the appearance of being at least ninety years old. Maybe more. The truck gave every indication of having been bequeathed to him by his father. But it got me to Doha, and mechanical assistance.

Having returned to the villa, I telephoned Mr Al-Khalifi to discover the degree of inconvenience I'd inflicted on him the previous night and to apologise for the trouble I'd caused.

'Oh, dear. I completely forgot about you. Did you have a problem?'

Kurt phoned to ask if I'd surreptitiously acquired a souvenir of my expedition. I was evasive, the telephone not always being the most secure form of communication in Qatar. But should he chance to visit the villa this week, there's something most interesting on the sideboard. And by any other name it smells as sweet.

✹ ✹ ✹ ✹ ✹

Scarface 2 died today. Frankly, I hadn't imagined it would upset me as much. Agreed he was just a tatty one-eyed, one-eared, emotional wreck, given to bursts of lengthy melancholy. But I'll miss him.

The washing machine killed him. For weeks now he'd taken to hunching theatrically on the top whenever it was in operation, gazing down for hours at my circulating socks and goat-chewed trousers. Whether the unceasing clatter or the frenzied vibrations seduced him, who knows?

I was working in the lounge when a bang from the kitchen was instantly followed by a complete loss of electrical power in the villa. The ensuing stench of burning rubber was accompanied by a veil of dense smoke which, once cleared, revealed the machine to be blackened, scorched and irreparably damaged. As was Scarface 2, lying motionless on the floor. The cause of the accident remains a mystery. The men from the Electricity Department came to replace a section of the wiring which had been destroyed. They suspected the whole washing machine had become 'live', electrocuting the cat, and considered it fortunate I wasn't touching the equipment myself at the time. They have a point.

The gloom of yesterday, like the scorched aroma, still hangs around the villa this morning. It's as if the livestock realise what happened.

Having spent a life without pets, I've never understood how readily we establish relationships with animals, although since moving to Qatar an awareness of them as individuals has undoubtedly developed, as has a curiosity.

I was watching the sheep ship discharging its cargo at the seaport recently and despite this being the sixth or seventh occasion, it still proved difficult to accept the conditions these animals endure. Every six weeks the ship arrives in Doha from Australia, crammed with around 70,000 live sheep. It's a vast floating cage divided into eight tiers, each one sub-divided into various pens with feeding and water troughs. As can be envisaged, given the combination of heat and the measure of excrement and urine, the smell is excruciating and discernible from some distance. How the Filipino crew abide it is beyond me. Eating accompanied by that stench must be abhorrent.

Yet my compassion is for the sheep. Around five per cent arrive dead after a journey of twenty days, whilst others, having cascaded downwards in the frantic crush through the discharging gangways, then find it impossible to ascend the ramp into the waiting trucks, due either to broken legs or general debilitation. These wretches are thrown in by the stevedores. Awaiting the appropriate paperwork, the sheep then remain in their wheeled cells, sometimes for hours, packed so tightly that individual movement is impossible. And more die standing up.

Being realistic, I imply no criticism of either the ship's crew or the Qatari authorities. Doubtless this is the method by which sheep, and the like, are transported throughout the world. But it disturbed me on first sight, and repetition has failed to diminish that feeling. Yes, I'm aware people travel on the London Underground and trains around Britain in overcrowded conditions, not dissimilar to those of the sheep trucks, often unable to turn without their movement synchronised with two dozen others. And yes, I eat meat, so I'm in no position to moralise. Oh, forget it.

An hour ago, I phoned Mr Al-Khalifi's maintenance supervisor to report last night's circumstances and to organise a replacement washing machine.

'I have big trouble with washing machine.'

'No problem. What trouble?'

'It blew up and killed the cat.'

'Oh, dear. So you need new cat or new washing machine? Washing machine take two weeks. Cat I get you tomorrow. What colour?'

Moira has just phoned.

'I hear you had a CATastrophe last night.'

Bloody Australians!

✳ ✳ ✳ ✳ ✳

Camels, mosques, the desert, men wearing white sheets with tablecloths on their heads, Qatar has many subjects to attract the amateur photographer. But as is frequently the case here, a complication exists. Photography is forbidden. Not completely you understand, as the authorities won't object if you snap a potted plant in your kitchen. Or even the cat in the garden. But anything more ambitious is firmly discouraged.

The explanation for this modesty is by the very nature of the subject difficult to establish. Maybe it's an ingenious device by those who matter to encourage speculation Qatar has something thunderously impressive to conceal. Like having an electronically-controlled garage but only a garden gnome to put in it.

However, undeterred by this negative stance, I decided to test the water, whilst recognising the gravity with which the authorities regard this issue – unlike one Frenchman who concluded it would be a splendid notion to photograph one of the 'Photography strictly forbidden' signs in Umm Said. That was four months ago. We haven't seen him since.

The simplistic view was to assume that if signs which forbid photography are erected in specific areas, then implicitly, where no such warnings prevail, it's out with the Instamatic. But as a precaution, to clarify the situation, I telephoned the British Embassy and spoke to the Ambassador. OK, to be honest, not literally the Ambassador, but his deputy the First Secretary. Or to be strictly accurate, the girl on the switchboard. It wasn't Barbie Doll. She's on holiday. She was advised last week her much coveted posting to America was postponed for a year. As a result she's taken two weeks unpaid leave in Wales to recuperate from the shock. But her replacement was most helpful and spoke to the First Secretary, who spoke to the Ambassador. The consensus of opinion was, providing areas with sign-posted restrictions are avoided, I should encounter no difficulty. Quite frankly I could have worked that out for myself. But it was reassuring to have the weight of the British Embassy behind me.

It was this morning at the Souq, the Arab's version of a car-boot sale, I elected to commence activities. So enter Peter Wood with camera. A bad move. Fifteen minutes later I was in a cell at the police station.

THE WASHING MACHINE WILL

Following a brief interval and an even briefer cup of tea, I was escorted to the interview room where eight policemen were involved in a communal argument. And believe me, for sheer intensity, a mass barney in Arabic surpasses anything this side of another Gulf War. On the wall hung a Rolf Harris Fun Mirror, cracked in several places and mottled with age. The faded Rolf Harris picture I could recognise, and, indeed, his didgeridoo. But it was less evident where the fun came in.

My camera was being transferred rapidly from one officer to another like a live grenade, prompting childhood memories of a 'pass the parcel' game. Obviously none of them fancied being caught in actual possession of the evidence when the sergeant appeared.

Moments later, carrying a cup of tea and a dejected-looking cat, the sergeant swept in. The music stopped. We got down to business. He was a man I knew, from a previous less contentious encounter, to be an ebullient, omnipotent character. Rumour has it that endorsed in the 'any distinguishing features' column of his passport is 'appendix scar on left side of nose'. Cool, calm and collected he isn't. But he has a sense of humour and, crucially, speaks some English.

Painstakingly, I described what I'd been doing and where I'd been doing it. This explanation appeared to coincide precisely with that of the three officers who'd arrested me. So no argument there. Nevertheless, before you could say Lord Lichfield, I was back in the cell.

No sooner had I made myself comfortable than the captain materialised and smiled at me through the bars. He was also known to me from the occasion last year I dozed off at the airport lights. He was presumably off-duty as his splendid uniform was not in evidence.

'Hello. Arsenal still play good.'

Allowing no time to determine whether this was a question or a statement, he continued.

'Don't worry. They know they were wrong, but it will take a few minutes to sort out in a satisfactory way.'

He smiled again and was gone.

Ten minutes later I found myself back upstairs in the interview room. The compromise proved a simple one. First the police would have the film developed and if it revealed no state secrets, I was free to go. This arrangement was one to which I readily agreed, having used twenty of the twenty-four exposures in the camera the previous week whilst photographing the villa and the livestock.

It took almost an hour for the roll of film to be developed. Then it was all handshakes, apologies and an assurance that discreet photography in the Souq area was permissible. Good.

Next Friday I intend returning to the Souq where I'll take twenty-three photographs with exceptional discretion. Then, who knows, I may wander along to a slightly more doubtful area, like outside the police station, with my camera in graphic evidence to suspicious eyes. If I play my cards right, I'll never again pay to have my films developed.

✳ ✳ ✳ ✳ ✳

According to BBC World Service news, a huge bomb left at Canary Wharf in London was defused by the Bomb Squad yesterday after five hours. This was just 300 yards from my home. It's too easy to forget such incidents from the relative safety of Qatar.

✳ ✳ ✳ ✳ ✳

It's intriguing to note that time in Qatar has an entirely different priority to that found in Britain. Remember the doughnuts? Quite simply there's appreciably more of it over here and dashing about will accomplish nothing. Far better to take your time – because everyone else will.

THE WASHING MACHINE WILL

To illustrate this – and I warn you it may take some while to get to the point – last week, whilst passing Mr Memnon Menon's cassette tape shop in Doha, I noticed a large sign on the door advising the premises was 'Closed for improvements'.

Inside there were signs of varied activity with three carpenters hammering and sawing, half a dozen electricians all surveying a strip-light, and two decorators sedately painting anything immobile – a potential hazard to the electricians.

Three days later I again drove by the shop. This time activity was noticeably more impressive, although the 'Closed for improvements' sign had partially fallen from the door and the premises was now 'Closed for imp'.

It was lunchtime yesterday, a further three days on, I next passed by. This time all work had ceased and the sign on the door now boldly advised, 'Grand re-opening, Tuesday'. However yesterday was Tuesday, but it was quite evident that no re-opening, grand or otherwise, was remotely imminent as the door remained firmly locked and the shop was empty and in darkness.

Turning to leave, I noticed Mr Memnon Menon across the street. He was in animated discussion with the driver of an open wagon, in the rear of which was crammed a group of bewildered-looking camels, all obviously as mystified as myself concerning the inactivity inside the shop.

I'd just come within smelling distance of the wagon when the proprietor noticed me and waved cheerily. I pointed back at the shop.

'When are you re-opening?'

'Tuesday.'

'But today is Tuesday.'

'Is it? Are you sure?'

Dashing across the road to his front door, he produced a large marking pen from his jacket pocket and with a single neat stroke crossed out 'Tuesday', and substituted 'Wednesday'.

169

IF THE SUN DOESN'T KILL YOU,

Let's hope so, I thought. I'm away to London for Christmas at the weekend and my MD has sent a list of cassette tapes he wants me to take back. So Wednesday would be my last opportunity to ingratiate myself with him, although frankly he could afford to buy them at full price in London. And where's my street-cred taking back a pile of Barry Manilow tapes? But the holiday will be welcome. Only ten days, but I'll enjoy it.

So this evening I once again returned to the shop for the re-opening, on this occasion with Moira who hoped to locate an early INXS album. (INXS are a popular Australian rock band, my lud.) During our doughnut evening, I remember Barbie Doll revealing she'd never heard of INXS. Or was it Australia?

We entered the shop, eagerly anticipating the improvements after the hectic activity of the previous seven days. But what a disappointment. It looked absolutely identical to the way it had been the week before. Even the 1985 calendar was still in the same position beside the door, although most of the dust which had accumulated since its year of origin had disappeared during the week's endeavours. It was clearly naïvely optimistic to have anticipated significant changes. But none whatsoever? And Mr Memnon Menon was wearing the same pair of orange, corduroy trousers I'd seen him in on every previous occasion.

'Hello, welcome to our new shop,' he said, beaming so broadly his glasses fell off and dropped with a plop into a rusty tin of dirty turpentine which was standing on the counter – the only apparent evidence of the previous week's events. Leaving him attempting to retrieve his glasses with a pair of broken scissors, and Moira to hunt for the INXS tape, I delved further into the shop. Did I mention Moira is married to a Qatari?

Unexpectedly, I found there had indeed been a change, as the cassette display racks were extended by about ten feet to the full length of the main wall and as they were already filled with tapes, an increased selection awaited my inspection.

By chance, on the previous day, the BBC World Service had broadcast some tracks from the new Elton John album which, despite the usual dreadful reception, I'd just managed to distinguish from on top of the kitchen table. As a result, I'd made a mental note to obtain the album in addition to the Barry Manilow tapes.

Having scanned the racks for the J section, which I failed to find, further investigation revealed all the tapes, about 5,000 in total, had been stacked quite haphazardly with no apparent regard to order. What a surprise!

Returning to the proprietor who was still probing the turpentine, I took hold of the tin and poured its contents into a conveniently placed bucket on the floor, neatly scooping the glasses into the palm of my hand before returning them to their owner. He thanked me, before indicating the bucket had a flawed bottom and I was now paddling in a pool of smelly, blue turpentine. But I pressed on.

'Mr Menon. Your cassette tapes don't appear to be stacked in any particular order and I can't find the one I want. It will take hours to sort through all these.'

'No problem. You just give me the name and I'll show you where it is.'

Ah, good, I thought. The man's obviously got some sort of indexing system, probably by code number, to identify the precise location of each tape.

'Elton John,' I said, and waited for him to reveal his sophisticated process for immediately locating the appropriate tape.

Writing the name on a piece of paper, he began walking to the far end of the rack.

'Elton John,' he repeated. 'No problem at all. I'll start looking at this end, and you can start looking at the other.'

So this man's idea of 'no problem at all', was to reduce a four hours search to about two hours. Around these parts, time isn't everything it's cracked up to be elsewhere, and when Dickens wrote 'Time and tide waited for no man', he'd clearly never set foot in Qatar.

✳ ✳ ✳ ✳ ✳

I've just given Kylie and Kurt a lift to the airport as they're off to Hamburg for Christmas. Barbie Doll came along with her knitting which she tackled vigorously throughout the journey. She's about halfway through an extension to the Doha ring road.

On the pavement outside the airport check-in area was an elderly man with an equally elderly sleeping dog which had a moneybox tied around its neck. Hanging from the box was a sign requesting donations for the Doha Animal Hospital. Kurt and I both dropped in a small contribution as the dog slept on, but no sooner had Kylie put ten riyals inside, than it instantly awoke and launched into a frenzied barking session, scaring the wits out of the poor girl. Kurt was so entertained by this he immediately thrust a further ten riyals into the box. The luckless Kylie was visibly upset and made an ill-considered attempt at retrieving her money. But the dog was having none of it.

Thereafter, despite her impending holiday, Kylie remained in a combative frame of mind, not improved by being laden with additional clothing in anticipation of her arrival in Hamburg, and the European winter. Colleagues here tell me the acclimatisation from heat to cold is more demanding than in the reverse direction, especially for an emaciated scrawn-bag like me. Doubtless I'll soon find out.

As they disappeared into passport control, Kylie was giving Kurt hell. God knows what about. He'd probably been breathing.

For a short while Barbie Doll and I sat in the car, my hands tentatively grasping her most prized possession. And if there's a more boring pursuit than holding a skein of wool while someone rolls it purposefully into a huge ball, for

172

heavens sake don't tell me. She also made another unexpected revelation, although on this occasion not one which will radically change my life. Her long-awaited transfer to America has been confirmed for the spring. And good luck to her. She's a nice girl and I'm sure deserves it.

As we drove from the airport, perspiring from the high evening humidity, the digital clock and thermometer which spans the exit road, revealed the current temperature in Doha to be minus 33° centigrade. And tomorrow I'll be in London – providing blizzards don't close Doha airport.

As a consequence of heavy traffic, driving Barbie Doll to her flat took longer than anticipated. By the time we arrived, she'd all but completed a mosque.

'In my end is my beginning, in my beginning is my end,' wrote Theodore Pluck. I can't imagine why.

14
Is this the beginning of civilisation as we know it?

I'm back from Christmas in London. I hadn't been inside the villa for more than ten seconds when I was assailed by an appalling commotion from outside. Prompt investigation revealed one of the goats pursuing a chicken up to the roof patio, presumably intent on eating the hapless creature. Finding itself trapped, the chicken obviously failed to appreciate its wings gave it a certain temporary advantage in such a situation and elected, instead, for the easy option – a massive rate of decibels to keep the goat at bay.

Disturbed by the uproar, the remaining goats emerged and registered their delight at my return by immediately scoffing my boots. I'd arranged for Mr Al-Khalifi to feed the livestock during my absence. The indications are that he may have omitted to do so.

Yes, it's good to be back. Whoops, my nose is on the move again.

Suddenly London seemed a very distant memory. But it was a good holiday. And hectic. I crammed in a Status Quo concert at Wembley, two good films in the West End, and *Tosca* at the Royal Albert Hall. (That place does remind me

174

of my late washing machine.) And to show I appreciate Christmas is a time of sacrifice and suffering, I watched both of Arsenal's holiday games. The one disappointment was a pop art exhibition at a gallery off Trafalgar Square. What lamentable hogwash – and they had the effrontery to charge five pounds. I couldn't pop art quick enough.

But the main event was the Christmas Eve wedding of my cousin Janet, and Stanford Gritt, a disc jockey who works for BBC World Service. The marriage was splendid but the reception was dreadful.

After Qatar, I found the weather in London numbingly cold. They were spot-on about the acclimatisation. On the first night it proved so bitter, that during an irrational dream involving Jeremy Beadle, I fell out of bed and snapped my pyjamas. (I got that from a cracker.)

Of course, the disadvantage of returning at Christmas after a lengthy period abroad, aside from discovering it costs almost a pound to travel one stop on London Underground, is most of your friends have no idea what to buy you for a present. So it's usually the easy option.

'Oh, a bottle of after-shave,' I shrieked with surprise after opening my seventh of the week. By the time Boxing Day arrived, socks had drawn nine-all with after-shave, with the latest Status Quo album defeating the new Chas and Dave by five copies to three. Heaven knows what I'll do with all the after-shave. Most of it will be incredibly Old Spice before I've waded through it.

One of the culprits is my cousin James whose birthday is on 26 December. Without wishing to appear ungrateful, why he's unable to come up with something more original once in a while is beyond me. After receiving an identical bottle from him for the third consecutive year, in addition to a precisely similar one for my birthday, I decided retaliation was due. I bought him a pair of socks this year and wrapped them separately. Christmas Day he got the left. On Boxing Day the right. Next year, if James buys me any more after-shave, he'll receive a pack of three batteries with a note 'Present not included'.

The most impractical gift I received was a soap-on-a-rope constructed in such an extraordinary shape as to render me speechless. It depicted a vintage car and was made with such precision, that had it not been 5 inches long and manufactured from soap, it would have been indistinguishable from the original. Mounted headlamps, spoke wheels, rear fitted spare tyre, caxton horn – undoubtedly a terrific piece of design and technical achievement, but totally useless for washing. Once wet, it zapped off at right angles when subjected to even the most amiable grip.

Quite why anyone should wish to invent soap-on-a-rope is beyond me. I see no conceivable advantage over ordinary soap other than if you inadvertently sit on it in the bath, you can always get it back.

Sadly, this wasn't the first occasion I'd seen this particular gift. In 1990 I'd despatched it to my second cousin George. And now, two years later, he had the effrontery to consign it back to me. It was my aunt and uncle in Milford Haven who first off-loaded it in my direction in 1989 as one of a pair, the other having long been jettisoned in exasperation.

So this soap was doing the rounds from one victim to the next, rather like an unwelcome chain-letter. Having received it from me, George had presumably taken one look and screamed 'Only someone with the intelligence of a retarded baboon could have sent me this' and chucked it in the nearest drawer. Then forgetting who'd sent it to him in the first place, he selected an appropriate sucker and it once again turned up in my possession. It appears to me that in some quarters the spirit of Christmas has deteriorated quite unacceptably.

The final evening of the holiday was spent at a variety show in the Hackney Empire, which, to my surprise, included a topless, female ventriloquist. No one seemed to notice if her lips moved.

*

After the relative organisation of London, my return flight quickly proved a symbolic reintroduction to the reality of life in Qatar.

Soon after boarding the aircraft the safety drill began, which these days is given on film rather than as a live demonstration. As it appeared on the screen, it was evident to even the most inexperienced traveller that the film was upside down, and it continued thus throughout its duration with none of the cabin staff apparently possessing either the knowledge, or the inclination, to correct it.

Shortly after take-off the in-flight movie began. It was *Strictly Ballroom*. Or, at least, it was *Strictly Ballroom* on the screen. Through the headphones it was *Home Alone 2* – a combination several of the passengers felt, not unreasonably, might impair their enjoyment of the film. The matter was soon brought to the attention of the cabin crew and after a meeting, and a short period of confusion, they sensibly abandoned the entire thing.

Then the stewardess appeared. It was lunchtime. I was offered an exhilarating choice of sliced beef or curried chicken, and after contemplation appropriate to the occasion, requested the beef. She handed me a foil tray from which I eagerly removed the lid. It was spaghetti. I hate spaghetti.

'Excuse me. You offered me beef or chicken and I've got spaghetti.'

'Really? We're not supposed to have that.'

Taking it back, she gave me a replacement tray from which I again removed the lid. It was a cheese salad. I hate cheese salad.

'Oh, dear,' the poor girl said, tearing the lids from three more trays to disclose a variety of meals, none of which were beef or, indeed, chicken. I eventually settled for a cod risotto. It was a decision I was soon to regret.

About an hour after the meal it became necessary to venture to the toilet. As I was sharing the aircraft with 240 other people, approximately sixty per cent of whom appeared to be under the age of five, not unexpectedly a small queue had formed. In fact, when I joined the queue we were just flying over Munich and we'd almost reached Istanbul before I got to the front.

Returning to my seat, I listed friends to whom I'd give after-shave lotion as Christmas presents next year. And then dozed off. I dreamt Michael Jackson had moved house. I found out after receiving one of those 'we've moved' cards. Weird. I don't remember giving him my address.

And apart from one of the passengers having a mild epileptic fit at three o'clock in the morning, and a wheel falling off the drinks trolley resulting in the virtual destruction of the tea urn and almost drowning everyone on board under three feet tall, the flight came to a rather uneventful conclusion.

As I entered the airport arrival lounge, a shout from across the relatively empty room alerted me to the rapidly approaching figure of the Thai assistant from the electrical shop. I'd not seen him since the trouble with my cassette player last year.

'Hello. Not see you long time. You been gone?'

'Yes. Just back from Christmas in London.'

He looked impressed.

'Is it good, London?'

'Oh, yes. But the weather's not as dry as Qatar.'

'Oh, dear. Does it rain much in France?'

Exit Wood left.

That wedding in London I referred to earlier. I admit it. It was a complete lie about the groom being a DJ for BBC World Service. I made that bit up, just for the joke about the dreadful reception. But the wedding reception was undeniably an ordeal.

After the tensions of the service, both families were

entombed in a frozen community hall with the very relatives they'd been trying to avoid for years.

The first problem was created by the hall chairs. The guests outnumbered them by at least two to one. This took practically an hour to resolve which seriously delayed the entrance of the celebration banquet. And no bad thing. I've never been that keen on curried rabbit and pineapple chunks.

Once the food had been eaten, or concealed under the table more likely, we endured a succession of dismal speeches, continually interrupted by sweet little boys in black satin suits hitting sweet little girls in pink cotton frocks. The bride's father then grabbed a microphone belonging to the disc jockey and burst into a twenty-five minute version of 'You'll Never Walk Alone', accompanied by a gang of half-stoned grandmothers in the corner. The bride's sister was then sick on the blancmange. Whether this was a consequence of her father's vocal endeavours, or would have happened anyway, who knows? What a start to married life.

Much earlier than expected, the bride and groom left the reception looking distinctly morose and claiming a six o'clock start for their honeymoon the following morning. Surly to bed, surly to rise.

* * * * *

It's the early hours of 1 January 1993, and time for reflection.

There's an old music hall adage which goes 'always leave 'em laughing'. Well bugger that. Reflective contemplation is inclined to be mainly circumspect.

Undoubtedly the past eighteen months has proved the most fulfilling period of my life. Like the kitchen of many a British take-away, Qatar is always liable to reveal more than you bargained for. They say about India, that after experiencing the culture shock, a Western visitor never returns from there the same person. For differing reasons, this place provokes a similar response. Life may not be as diverse or sophisticated as in Britain, and things can occasionally take a little longer to accomplish than might be deemed ideal. But without wishing to sound like the Archbishop of Canterbury, this environment encourages reconsideration of priorities and aspirations. Perspectives change. Twice a week at the pub, *Eastenders*, and following Arsenal, seem less essential than before. Nothing is more important in Qatar than the next day. And that's important.

During the past eighteen months I've made observations which haven't always demonstrated Qatar as being the Utopia we all seek. Doubtless there are those here who have been offended by these. They shouldn't be. Whilst organisation and efficiency are sometimes of unconvincing quality – so what! Few examples can claim significance when compared with some of the inconveniences of Western life. What does a barmy driving test matter when you know your car won't be stolen the following day? What does the odd blown-up cooker matter when you know the IRA won't try the same trick on you in the street? What does censored television matter when you know some witless yob won't yell mindless obscenities at you through the screen? Jesus. I am beginning to sound like the Archbishop of Canterbury. True, there are examples of disorganisation around the place as I'm sure Qatar would be first to confirm. Indeed, I'd be second. But no reservations about the life from me.

Before the middle of this century, the country depended on fishing and, predominantly, pearling for its existence. Its people were poor, a situation exacerbated by competition from the newly developed Japanese cultured pearl industry. Then came oil. Suddenly Qatar no longer found itself locked in the past but hurtling towards the twenty-first century. In less than forty years, the country has seen progress which elsewhere has taken centuries to achieve and its citizens and methods have been confronted with the daunting task of matching this progress despite the country's natural handicaps. And do they have a couple of those!

There's a joke concerning our neighbours across the channel. The problem with France is it's a lovely country but full of French. The converse applies to Qatar. Full of terrific people, but stuck with a landscape with even less appeal than eating spinach.

The natural Qatari terrain consists entirely of a sand and rock desert so flat that standing on an After Eight mint gets you the best view around. And with an average annual rainfall of 2 inches, and only three per cent of the land naturally cultivable, what chance is there of providing an agreeable lifestyle for the residents? More than you might think.

In 1956, the population of Qatar was 26,000 – now it has increased an astonishing sixteen-fold; prior to 1956, the country had no schools or education system – now free single-sex schooling, which includes a modern university, is available to everyone, Qatari or non-Qatari, and illiteracy has tumbled from eighty-one to twenty-two per cent; in 1986, a programme aimed at achieving self-sufficiency in food production was begun – now, assisted by modern desalination plants, cultivable land has increased four-fold; the Hamad Hospital in Doha, which opened in 1982, is regarded as one of the most eminent in the Gulf region, offering free treatment to everyone; public gardens and ornamental roundabouts have recently been constructed, and the corniche in Doha with its spectacle of traditional mosaics, is accepted as one of the most impressive attractions in the Gulf – like so many of Qatar's accomplishments, benefiting not only its own nationals, but equally its majority non-Qatari population. Even during my brief residency in the country, visible evidence of this progression abounds. Qatar seems to improve almost by the day.

Taken in collaboration with the state's heavy industrial

development, that's no bad record. Yes, it has the asset of a relatively small population in comparison to its oil income, which has become a decisive factor. And yes, it enjoys the benefits from importing a sizeable and cheap labour force. But other countries with similar advantages have not always used them as effectively.

The Al-Thani family has presided over Qatar as an absolute monarchy since the nineteenth century, without legislature or political parties. Whatever your opinion of hereditary rule, certainly in less populous countries it has more going for it than might initially be imagined. And there's no evidence anyone else here believes they can do better. Quite the contrary. Most independent observers regard the rule of the Emir as astute, given both the state's unprecedented recent development and its constituent population. Many countries have found rapidly changing internal circumstances, combined with a high proportion of foreign residents, to be a source of unrest and political instability. But not Qatar.

With the state now giving serious thought to opening itself to controlled tourism, the very individual appeal of the place could legitimately tempt the more intrepid sightseers. (No bikinis, lager louts, or Spurs supporters, please.) But what would they find? Nothing to support the scarcely complimentary impressions of past travellers.

In 1865, Palgrave described Qatar as the land God forgot, and the then main town of Bida as the miserable capital of a miserable country. In 1954, Sir Rupert Hay claimed it to be the ugliest stretch of territory that God has created. Had he never been to Blackburn?

But today Doha is a modern city which thankfully retains the best of its cultural origins and neither Palgrave or Hay, in the unlikely event of their ever revisiting the country, unlikely as they're both dead and wouldn't get an entry visa anyway, could now justify their previous assertions.

THE WASHING MACHINE WILL

Just forty years ago Qatar was wholly dependent on its neighbours. Food, together with all other essentials, were imported – even the wood for building boats. Slaves, brought originally from East Africa during the nineteenth century for the pearling industry, still existed in many households. Contrast that with the certainty that within a few years, the State of Qatar will enjoy one of the highest per capita incomes in the world, far exceeding that of the United Kingdom. But enough. I'm sounding like the Qatari Tourist Office.

Now an apology. But to whom? The nominations are – Kylie; *The Gulf Times*; The Albanian Dance and Accordion Group; Qatar.

And the award goes to – and those not wishing to know the result should look away now – *The Gulf Times*. In recognition of all those cheap jibes I've made. Yes, it's still the most boring newspaper in the world, but I should acknowledge the constraints under which it's produced and the environment for which it caters. No chance of 'Freddie Starr ate my camel' here. Just facts, facts, yesterday's weather forecast, and more facts – which, having seen some of the British nationals over the holiday period, may not be altogether a bad thing. And yes, I appreciate it only prints the weather information as it's received from the appropriate authoritative source. But why does that seem to be the local butcher? And one last thought on the subject. If anyone was to enquire why a newspaper I repeatedly assert to be the most dreary in the world, appears to occupy such an inordinate amount of my time and interest, then what could I say? Apart from bugger off.

And now it's time to roll the credits. Tim said that at the end of one of his programmes. Slick, eh?

With the Allied Forces again threatening to attack Iraq, there were indications of increased military activity and tighter security when I arrived back in Qatar this afternoon, for probably the last time. Work on the North Field Project is ahead of schedule and there's unlikely to be opportunity for further time away before my responsibilities are completed towards the end of this summer.

During the past hour, two telephone calls have disturbed my reflections. The first was good news. Vincent is out. It came from Mr Memnon Menon. I was unaware he knew Vincent but, as it transpires, he is his cousin. Released from jail, with no explanation, six days before Christmas, he was taken straight to the airport for deportation. It's a relief – at least lengthy imprisonment has been avoided. Mr Memnon etc. gave me Vincent's home address. I'll keep in touch.

The second call was just moments ago from Mr Al-Khalifi. He phoned to wish me a happy new year, and for some reason best known to himself, suggested I give thought to writing a book relating my experiences in Qatar. Laughing, I said it was a daft idea. But it could make a good board-game.

Mr Al-Khalifi also pointedly enquired whether I intend implementing any new year resolutions. He has the opinion I've not always made sufficient effort to integrate into the Qatari lifestyle and this year I should consider adapting my traditional English attitude. He's bang on, of course. I can still master only a few phrases of Arabic, shameful when the Vincents of this world can converse to some degree in both English and Arabic, in addition to their own tongue.

But I won't change. Agreed I've not always slipped imperceptibly into a way of life which can sometimes be puzzling. But what's life without an element of mystery on occasions? Like why did the entire world arrive at Marks & Spencer's refund desk in Oxford Street on 28 December, thirty seconds before me and my nine bottles of after-shave? But no matter. It's usually been fun and invariably compelling. True, regrets I've had a few but then again too few to mention. I did what I had to do and saw it through without exemption. I've lived a life that's full and travelled each and every highway. And more, much more than this, I did it my way. That's Shakespeare, isn't it?